It was ridiculous. It was insane. But I could not help myself. I had to find that figure and take it back to Professor Jarvis. Wildly I jerked open the top drawer of the bureau and began to rummage inside. I felt along both sides and under the piles of clothing. Then I removed the whole drawer and set it on Julia's bed and threw everything out of it.

The wax dog, if that was indeed what the figure had been, was gone, but I did find something else, so flat and thin against the base of the drawer that I would never have located it by touch alone. It was a photograph of me, one of the discards from the set of snow pictures that Mother had printed the month before. The face and body were covered with what appeared to be splotches of bright red paint.

LOIS DUNCAN is the author of over thirty best-selling books for young people and adults. Her novels have won her high acclaim and many have been chosen as ALA Best Books for Young Adults and Junior Literary Guild selections. Her most recent novel for Delacorte Press was *Don't Look Behind You*. Among her most popular suspense stories for young people are *The Twisted Window*, *Killing Mr. Griffin*, *Stranger with My Face*, *Summer of Fear*, *Daughters of Eve*, *Locked in Time*, *Down a Dark Hall*, *Ransom*, and *The Third Eye*, all available in Dell Laurel-Leaf editions.

Lois Duncan is a full-time writer and a contributing editor to *Woman's Day* magazine. She lives with her family in New Mexico.

Summer of Fear

Lois Duncan

Published by
Dell Publishing
a division of
Bantam Doubleday Dell Publishing Group, Inc.
666 Fifth Avenue
New York, New York 10103

ISBN: 0-440-98324-X
RL: 5.8

Reprinted by arrangement with Little, Brown and Company,
Inc.

Printed in the United States of America
One Previous Edition
September 1990

35   34   33   32   31   30   29   28   27

RAD

for Louise

Summer of Fear

One _____

It's summer. Summer—again.

I go out this morning to get the paper and although it is still early, barely eight o'clock, the sun is warm on my hair and on the back of my neck, promising the heat of the coming day.

I pick up the paper, roll off the rubber band, and begin leafing through, standing there in the front yard with the thin rays of the sun on my back and the dew on the grass already drying beneath my feet.

I find it at last on page seven of section C. Usually, if I look long enough, it is there, a story that fits. Sometimes it is only a few lines, one of those filler items they use when the big stories aren't long enough to reach the bottom of the page. Other times it is a real article with a photograph, as it is today.

A family—parents, their teenage daughter and an unidentified girl friend—are missing, believed lost in the San Andres Mountains west of Alamogordo. They went for a week's camping trip and now, ten days later, they haven't returned. There is a picture of the family—the couple, handsome, outdoorsy looking people about the age of my own parents, and the pretty, laughing daughter. It was evidently taken just before a hike for they are all wearing packs, and in the background there is a camper. Did the "girl friend" who accompanied them take the picture? It seems strange otherwise that she is not shown.

"We found the camera at a picnic area at the foot of the mountain," a state trooper is quoted as saying. "We assume the family may have been camping there. However, there is no sign of the camper truck or of any of the other belongings. It's very strange."

It's strange too, it seems to me, that the girl friend is "unidentified." Why hasn't her own family reported that she is missing? Might it be that she has no family, no place of belonging? Where did she come from and how does she fit into the lives of these beautiful people? Is she with them now, sharing their ordeal, or is she somewhere else, quite alone, thinking back upon them and smiling a little as she drives a camper truck along the highway? Why wasn't she in the picture with the others?

Standing here on the lawn, I look at the photograph and read the article. I read it again. So often, when I pick up the paper on sweet summer mornings, I find an article such as this one, and I can't help asking myself . . . who is this person? Could it be . . . ? Is it . . . ?

* * *

It has been four years now since that summer. I am not yet rid of it. Perhaps I never will be. Thinking back, I can even place the beginning of it all, the very day. It was June second. School was just out and spring just over and the real summer not yet started.

On that morning of June second I lay in bed, watching the sun slant through between the slats in the venetian blind, feeling lazy and a little guilty because the rest of them were up, and downstairs. I could hear them and I could smell the breakfast coffee. The odor of frying bacon drifted up the stairwell and seeped through the crack under the bedroom door.

If it had been a weekday my mother probably would have gotten me up even though it was summer. She liked to get breakfast over with and the kitchen clean so she could use the sink for rinsing her photographs. But on Saturdays she was easier going and if we were lucky we got to sleep.

I stretched and yawned and closed my eyes and opened them again, reveling in my laziness. Then the phone rang.

It rang twice more and became silent. Suddenly alert, I lay, waiting for the sound of footsteps on the stairs and somebody's voice calling, "Rachel? It's for you!"

When moments passed and the sounds didn't come I yawned again and swung my legs over the side of the bed and got up.

My jeans were tossed across the back of a chair by the window. I put them on along with a halter top and, reaching over, pulled the cord that adjusted the blinds so I could look out at the yard below. The grass was soft and green, almost long enough to be mowed. Until this year the mowing had been Peter's job, but now that he was eighteen and working it had been decided that the job would descend to Bobby. Bobby was eleven and small for his age. It was hard to imagine him pushing the rotary mower over the whole length of the yard.

Along the back fence the roses were beginning to bud, and on the far side of the fence I could see Mike Gallagher watering his mother's vegetable garden. Leaning close to the screen, I pursed my lips and let out a long, shrill whistle. Mike started, lifted his eyes to focus upon the window, and raised a hand in a gesture of greeting. Then he pointed toward the sky, and I nodded vigorously, hoping he could see me. The pool at the Coronado Club had just opened for the summer and the day before we had discussed the possibility of going swimming if the weather was good. Now, in sign language, Mike was saying, "It looks perfect!" and I was answering, "Great! Let's go!"

The Gallaghers had lived next door for as long as I could remember, but it was only during the past year that Mike and I had become aware of each other as more than casual neighbors. Now, gazing down at the blond head bent again to the watering, I found myself smiling.

He needs a haircut, I thought with a happy feeling of possessiveness. It wasn't a criticism. I liked his hair shaggy.

Turning away from the window I paused before the mirror that hung over the bureau in order to run a comb through my own short tangle of reddish hair. It bounced back immediately into a mop of uncontrollable curls. In the era of long, smooth, straight hair, those curls were the bane of my existence. I wrinkled my nose in disgust and decided not to bother trying to improve myself further. What was the use of putting on makeup if you were going swimming?

I left the room and went downstairs to breakfast.

To my surprise, there was no one in the kitchen. They had been there recently I could tell, for the coffee was perking on the back of the stove and bacon lay draining on a paper towel on the counter top. Eggs and bread sat out in preparation for the usual Saturday meal of French toast, and the morning paper was spread open to the sports page on the kitchen table.

"Mother?" I called. "Dad?"

Then I became conscious of sounds from the living room, a soft, choking noise and my father's voice, low and consoling. Hurrying through the kitchen, I shoved open the door that led into the next room.

They were there, the four of them. My parents were seated on the sofa, and Mother was crying, her hands over her face. Dad had his arm around her, and the two boys were standing awkwardly, looking down at them, as though not knowing what ought to be done or said.

"What is it?" I cried as panic hit me. I couldn't remember ever having seen my mother cry.

It was Bobby who answered.

"It's Aunt Marge and Uncle Ryan," he said. "They're dead."

"Dead!" I caught my breath at the dreadful word. My stomach lurched, but it was more from

shock than grief. I had seen my aunt and uncle
only once when I was little and it was too long ago
for me to remember. Since my early childhood they
had lived in a series of strange places, and in recent years they had made their home in an isolated
area of the Ozarks where Uncle Ryan wrote his
novels and Aunt Marge worked at her painting.

"All these years," Mother sobbed, "and we never
visited! We should have insisted that they come
last Christmas!"

"You can't insist on something like that," Dad
said gently. "Ryan was tied up in his writing. You
couldn't have budged him from that mountain wil-
derness for anything, and Marge never wanted to
be anyplace that he wasn't. As for our going there
—we weren't invited."

"We could have invited ourselves," Mother said
"We were family, the only family Marge had. It
didn't matter whether Ryan wanted us or not."

"It did matter," Dad said. "Ryan didn't want
people around when he was working, and Marge
went along with him on everything. To have arrived on their doorstep uninvited would have been
unthinkable. Besides, we expected to see them this
summer."

"What happened?" I asked, unable to withhold
the question. "How were they killed?"

"In a car wreck," Peter told me. He stood
hunched forward, his hands in his pockets, and I
could tell from the unaccustomed gruffness of his
voice that he was shaken as I was by the sudden-
ness of tragedy. "It happened yesterday, but the
message didn't come till this morning. They were
driving the woman who worked for them back to

her home in the village, and the car went off the side of a cliff. It burned."

"How awful!" I gasped. I tried not to envision the scene, to let it be words in my mind instead of a picture, but this was impossible. A car burning at the base of a cliff—my aunt and uncle and another woman inside it—

"Awful," I whispered and went to sit by Mother. "Did you say we were going to see them this summer?"

"We hoped to," Dad said. "Marge wrote at Christmas that when Ryan's new novel was completed they planned, as she put it, to 'come back to civilization for a while.' Marge wanted to have Julia with them for her senior year instead of off at boarding school."

"Julia," Mother said softly. "That poor child." She lowered her hands from her face and turned to my father. "We'll have to go get her immediately. Imagine her being there all alone through such a terrible time!"

"The sheriff's telegram said she was staying at the house," Dad said, "and since they don't have a phone I don't suppose there's any way to get in touch with her except with a return telegram. By the time that's delivered we could be there ourselves."

"She must just have gotten back from boarding school," Mother said. "Marge was so looking forward to having her come home. She must have been lonely, living so far from everyone, with Ryan buried in his work." Her voice shook, threatening to break again. "She had no one, you know. No one but me. We were the last of our side of the family."

"How old is Julia now?" Dad asked. "Fifteen or sixteen?"

"A little older than that," Mother said. "I remember when she was born Peter was just a toddler. She's seventeen, two years older than Rachel."

"You're right about our needing to get her," Dad said. "I'll call the airport and see what sort of flight we can get and then write this Sheriff Martin to get a message to her. I suppose our best bet would be to get a plane to Springfield and rent a car there. Do you recall the name of the village nearest to where they lived?"

"Pine Crest," Mother said. "That's where they got their mail, but their house must be quite a way from there because Marge wrote once that they only drove down to pick up their letters once a week when they did their grocery shopping. Call now, Tom, please. There's no time to waste."

My father got to his feet and went into the hall where the wall phone hung. I reached over and patted Mother's hand.

"Shall we all go?" I asked.

"No, dear. I think not." Mother shook her head as though trying to focus her thoughts. "It will be an exhausting trip, especially if we have to drive from Springfield, and there will be so much to be done so quickly. It will work best if you'll stay here and run the house for Peter and Bobby. You'll have Mrs. Gallagher to turn to if there are any problems." Her voice shook. "I can't believe it! Margy —dead! We had a tree house once."

I squeezed her hand. At least she wasn't crying any longer.

Bobby said, "Are you going to bring that girl home with you?"

"Your cousin Julia? Yes, of course, if she's willing to come. I can't imagine where else she would go. There are no other relatives."

"Should I remember her?" Peter asked. "I've got a feeling I saw her once."

"You did. It was the year you started the first grade. Ryan was off somewhere getting interviews for some articles he was writing, and Marge came to us for a couple of weeks with Julia. She was a darling little thing, and as I remember, you teased her terribly. She had a toy rabbit, and you took it away from her and gave it to Rachel, and she chewed a hole in its ear."

The memories kept coming, flashing across the screen of my mother's mind, filling her voice with grief. We stayed there close to her, the boys and I, listening, for that was the only comfort we knew how to give.

At last Dad came back into the room.

"We can get a noon flight," he said. "I don't know how long we'll need to stay so I just made reservations one way. We'll arrange the return flight later."

"I'd better go pack," Mother said. "Bob, will you get my overnight bag down from the attic? Peter, you'd better leave for work; you're already late." She paused, refocusing her mind with effort. "Oh, dear, nobody's had breakfast!"

"Don't worry about that," I told her. "We're none of us hungry. If anyone wants anything, there's dry cereal."

Mother and Dad went upstairs and Peter left the house and Bobby went up to the attic. I went out to the kitchen and put away the eggs and bread and took the bacon, cold and dry on its greasy towel, and put it in the plastic food bowl for my dog Trickle. I poured coffee into two mugs and took them up to my parents who were in their room taking things out of the bureau. Then I went back downstairs and wandered from room to room, feeling useless because there was really nothing to be done.

Finally I went outside.

Mike was coming up the walk. He was wearing his swimming trunks and a T-shirt and had a towel tossed over his shoulder. He grinned, and I felt shocked for a moment until I remembered that he didn't know.

"Hey, Red," he said. "You're not ready."

"I can't go," I told him. "We've had a tragedy. My aunt and uncle were killed in a car wreck."

"Oh—tough." The smile left his face and his blue eyes lost their sparkle. "I'm sorry, Rae."

"Aunt Marge was my mother's only sister," I said. "My folks are leaving this afternoon. It happened in Missouri."

"Tough," Mike said again. "Your mom must be all broken up."

"She is," I said. "She and Dad are going to go there to take care of things or—well, whatever you do at a time like this. They're going to bring my cousin back with them. Her name's Julia."

"Julia," Mike repeated. "I don't think I've ever heard you talk about her. Is she going to live with you?"

"I don't know," I said. "For a while, I guess. She's seventeen; that's too young to be off on her own." Until he asked this I had not thought about Julia's living with us in a permanent fashion, only visiting for a while until other plans could be made for her. But what other plans might there be for a teenage girl with no other living relatives?

"It'll be like getting a sister, won't it?" Mike said. "It's crazy, isn't it, thinking you'll never have anything but two brothers and then finally, at your age, getting a sister."

"Crazy," I echoed with a faint stirring of uneasiness. What would it be like to share my home and my family with a ready-made sister whom I didn't even know?

Two _____

Julia. How many times I was to repeat that name to myself in the days that followed before my parents' return from their sad errand to the Ozark Mountains. *Julia.* It would come into my head at the oddest times—when I was ironing a blouse—scrubbing potatoes to put in the oven—sitting with a book in the lawn chair in the backyard. Who is Julia, really? What does she look like? What kind of person is she, this girl who is going to be my almost-sister?

Peter thought he could remember her a little. I could not remember her at all. Since her mother and mine had been sisters, I wondered if she would have some sort of resemblance to Mother. Mother was little and freckled with an animated face and curly, carrot-colored hair that would never go the way she wanted it. Peter and I had inherited that hair. Bobby, on the other hand, though he was slightly built, had the smooth blond hair and handsomely featured face of our father.

Julia. It was a pretty name. I tried to remember the things I had heard about Julia over the years. I knew, of course, that she went to a boarding school in New England because there were no good public schools in the area of her mountain home. I had a feeling that she was supposed to have a talent of some kind. What was it she did—sing? Paint? Write poetry? To tell the truth, I had never been interested enough to make note of it or of anything else much in the way of dull, family chitchat in Aunt Marge's annual Christmas letters.

But now I did want to know. I wanted to prepare myself.

"Why do you have to be prepared?" Mike asked logically. "She'll be what she is, period. You'll find out soon enough."

We were sitting in the backyard, eating ham sandwiches and playing with Trickle. Somehow eating out in back with the sunlight falling in patches between the branches of the elm tree made it seem more definite that vacation was here. Trickle was rolling around on his back, asking to have his stomach tickled, but actually waiting to see if a piece of ham might fall out of one of the sandwiches.

"I'll have to share my room with her," I said. "I've always had my own room, you know. It will seem funny, having a stranger living there with me."

"She won't be a stranger long," Mike said. "I should think you'd like it, having another girl around. It'll make one more voice to add to the racket when the gaggle gets together."

By "the gaggle" he meant me and my best friend Carolyn Baker. He liked to tell us that when we started chattering we made as much noise as a gaggle of geese.

"I hate that word," I told him irritably. "There's nothing goosey about us. Carolyn and I are friends because we picked each other. We have things in common. It's different just to have somebody thrust upon you. What if she giggles all the time and spits through her teeth when she talks and likes to go to bed at nine o'clock?"

"I hardly think she'll have much to giggle about," Mike reminded me, and I felt my face grow hot as I realized the stupidity of my statement.

"Of course not," I said. "That was a dumb thing to say. I'm being horrid."

Mike didn't contradict me. He broke off a piece of his sandwich and gave it to Trickle who slurped it down as though he hadn't been fed for a week.

"I've got to get going," he said. "I promised Professor Jarvis I'd cut his grass for him this afternoon. You want to go to a show or something tonight? There's a Dustin Hoffman film at the Lobo."

"I guess so," I said. "But I hate to leave Bobby rattling around by himself. Pete's usually got a rehearsal or something in the evening and with the folks gone—"

"Bring him along," Mike said. "I'll pick you both up at seven-thirty."

He went home, not bothering to go around to the front but putting both hands on the top of the fence and vaulting over. A moment later I heard the creak of his garage door as he opened it to get out the lawn mower. Professor Jarvis's house was next door to the Gallaghers' on the other side, so cutting that lawn was a simple process.

Suddenly the yard was empty and the world was very still. I picked up the pop cans and carried them across the yard and into the kitchen. The house was so quiet I could hear the clock ticking on the kitchen wall.

It occurred to me how seldom it was that I was alone in the house even for a few hours, much less a whole afternoon. Mother was almost always there cooking or sewing or printing pictures in the little darkroom Dad had rigged up for her out of the storeroom in the garage.

I set the cans down on the counter and went to the telephone and dialed Carolyn's number. The phone was answered on the second ring.

"Hi," I said. "Want to do something? Pete's at work and Bobby's out on his bike somewhere and I'm about to go stir crazy."

"Great," Carolyn said. "Come on over."

"What are you doing?" I asked suspiciously. I had heard that tone in her voice before.

"Washing walls," Carolyn said brightly. "You can sit and talk to me."

"Thanks, but no thanks." I knew Mrs. Baker. When she went on a cleaning spree nobody in the house was spared. All you had to do was walk in the door and you found yourself with a sponge in one hand and a can of wall cleaner in the other.

"When are your folks coming home?" Carolyn asked. "Have you heard anything from them?"

"Not a word. They said they'd call when they knew what was happening. They drove the T-Bird to the airport and left it there, so they won't have to be picked up."

"They'll probably call tonight then. Look, I've got to hang up. The wall's drying in streaks and

Mom'll kill me. No—worse than that—she'll make me do it over. Okay?"

"Okay," I said. "Have fun. So long."

I put the phone back on the hook and then just stood there, wondering what to do with myself. I was so used to having people around me that I hardly knew where to begin with self-entertaining. I wondered if Julia was a sociable person, somebody you could really talk to. I wondered what her interests were.

If only I could remember the things Aunt Marge had written in that Christmas letter. I should have read it more carefully, but at the time it arrived I had not thought it important. Where was it now, I wondered. Long gone with the Christmas wrappings and dried pine needles, or was it possible that it was still around somewhere? Mother often kept Christmas cards, especially the ones that contained photographs or personal messages. Perhaps Aunt Marge's letter was among them.

With a feeling of relief at having found an afternoon activity, I went upstairs and opened the door of the linen closet. We had the sort of house where things were not always where they should be. Our sheets were kept in a spare chest in Bobby's room, and the linen closet was used to store things we didn't know what to do with. Mother kept her negative file there and Dad his *National Geographics*, and there were boxes of things that didn't work any longer, like broken hair dryers and flashlights without switches and games with parts missing.

On the second shelf I found a cardboard box labeled "Christmas Cards." When I opened it, the card from Aunt Marge and Uncle Ryan was right on top.

It was a homemade card, not a glossy, commercial one, and the painting on the front was one that Aunt Marge had done herself. It was a picture of an angel singing on a mountain top. I had seen it when it had arrived, but had not paid much attention. Aunt Marge had always made the family cards. Now, because I knew it was the last card we would ever receive from her, I sat down on the floor at the base of the closet and really studied it.

Aunt Marge had talent, that was apparent. The sweet face of the angel glowed with a special sort of joy; her hair fluffed out about her head in a dark brown halo and the blue eyes seemed an echo of the sky. Even I, who knew little about art, could tell that the hand that had held the paint brush had moved with love.

I opened the card. There was no printed greeting. Aunt Marge had filled the space with a handwritten message:

Dearest family—

Christmas again and joy abounds! Our angel Julie is home for the holidays and the house is filled with singing! What a contrast to the last few months with Ryan deep in the rewrite of his novel and no one to talk to most of the day except Sarah Blane. Sarah's a local who has been working for us since last fall—pleasant to have another female in the house but hardly a replacement for J. Hopefully things will be different next spring. Once Ryan's book is finished he has agreed to come

back to civilization so that we may have Julie
with us for her senior year. And the first thing
on the agenda will be a visit with you! I can't
believe that Peter has graduated and Rachel
is in high school, and I have never even seen
Bobby. How life does manage to get away
from us! Have a beautiful Christmas. The
photo of the children is gorgeous, Leslie. You
must take some of J when we are together
again.

Much, much love—*Marge*.

The line that stopped me was, "How life does
manage to get away from us." In view of what
came after, it seemed so ironic. But I forced myself past it to the final loving words, and when I
finished them I found myself with tears in my eyes
and a tight feeling in my throat. How could a person one minute be this vitally alive—writing, painting, making joyful plans—and be gone the next?
The love and closeness that must have existed between mother and daughter showed plainly in every line. How lost Julia must feel now, how dread-
fully lonely!

She'll need us, I thought, more than anybody's
ever needed anyone before. What a horrid person
I must be, worrying about something as small as
sharing my room. I'll like Julia—in fact, I'll *love*
her. I'll be a real sister to her, not just a cousin. I'll
do everything I can to see that she's happy here.
If only I—

I was startled from my thoughts by the sound of
a door opening in the hall below. It must be Bobby,
I thought—and then, through the emptiness of the

house, a familiar voice called, "Hello! Is anybody home?"

"Mother!" I scrambled to my feet, the Christmas note still clutched in my hand. "I'm here—up here!"

I went down the stairs two at a time. Mother was standing in the downstairs hallway, and Dad was coming through the door with two suitcases in his hands. My eyes took in the weariness of my mother's face, and I threw my arms around her in a hard hug.

"I didn't think you'd be back so soon!"

"There was no funeral," Mother said. "There—wasn't need for one. We decided to have a memorial service here instead. And there weren't very many things to be packed. Marge and Ryan hadn't collected a lot of material things."

There was a tremor in her voice and she hugged me back with an intensity that showed the strain the past few days had put upon her.

"How are things here?" she asked. "Has everything gone along all right? Where are the boys?"

"Pete's working," I said, "and Bob's off biking. Everything's been fine, but we've missed you. I'm so glad you're home."

"We're glad, too," Mother said. She loosened her arms from around me and stepped back to reach out a hand to the girl who was standing behind her, a girl I had not even seen, shadowed as she was by my father's form in the doorway.

She was a plain, thin girl with long, black hair that hung halfway to her waist. Her brows were heavy, her face narrow and sallow, but her *eyes*— even now, thinking back upon that moment, I cannot begin to describe my first impression of her eyes. They were deep and dark and filled with secrets. Haunted eyes. Haunting eyes. They were the strangest eyes I had ever seen.

"Rachel," Mother said with a special gentleness in her voice, "this is Julia."

Three _____

"Hi," I said. "I'm Rachel." And I thrust out my hand.

It was not the way I had meant to greet her. Instantly I wished I could go back and redo the greeting and at the very least turn it into a hug. It was just that she was so far from what I had expected.

"Hello," Julia said and, after an instant's hesitation, put her hand in mine. It was a thin hand but surprisingly strong.

"Call me Rae," I said awkwardly. "That's what my friends call me. I'm so sorry about your family. It's so awful. We're *all* so sorry."

"I know," Julia said. "Thank you."

"You're going to be sharing Rachel's room," my father said, setting one suitcase on the floor and putting his free arm around Julia's shoulders. "Let me take your bag up and you can start getting settled."

"I'd like that," Julia said. "I am a mite tired." Her

voice was low-pitched, more like a woman's voice than a young girl's. When she said "like" it sounded more like "lack," and "tired" like "tarred."

"Of course you are, dear," Mother said warmly. "It would be a miracle if you weren't. Why don't you go up and lie down for a while? There's no rush about unpacking."

"That's a good idea," Dad said. "A little rest never hurt anybody. Come on, honey, I'll show you the way." With Julia's suitcase in one hand and with the other arm still protectively around her, he steered her up the stairs.

Mother and I stood silent, listening to the sound of their footsteps in the upstairs hall. Then Mother sighed.

"Oh, it's good to be home!"

"I'll bet it is," I said. "It must have been dreadful."

"Painful," Mother said. "That's a better word. It was so painful, seeing that home for the first time, and Marge not in it. It was a lovely home, Rae, small and simple and rustic but perched on the side of a mountain where the breeze blew straight through one set of windows and out another. Marge had flowers planted everywhere, and her paintings were on all the walls. Her easel was set up in the bedroom with a canvas half finished, and her work smock was tossed on the bed as though she'd just run out for a moment and would be right back. And Ryan had left a page of his novel in his typewriter."

We went into the living room and Mother dropped her purse on the coffee table and sat down on the sofa. I sat on the chair across from her.

"You said there wasn't a funeral?" I asked.

"There was nothing to bury," Mother said. "The car had burned. There was only a shell of metal left. At least, it must have been fast, it fell so far. Those winding roads—the sheer drop-offs—it's incredible. And Julia wanted to leave as soon as possible. She said there was nothing to stay for.

"Dad went down to Pine Crest and listed the house with the man who runs the little grocery store. He seemed to be the one who handles all real estate sales in that area. And we left the furnishings in it. We packed all the personal things into boxes and left them at Springfield to be shipped. I think Julia will want to have them someday when the grief has had time to lessen."

"How is she taking it?" I asked.

"Surprisingly well. Almost too well, actually. I think she's still in a state of shock." Mother shook her head worriedly. "It was a shattering experience for her. Her parents had left for what was to be only a couple of hours, just long enough to drive the girl Sarah back to the village for the weekend and to pick up some groceries and the mail. Julia had decided against going with them because she had a little headache and wanted to take a nap. She says that when she woke up it was getting dark and her parents weren't back. She started dinner, and when it was cooked they still hadn't returned. She sat up waiting for them all night."

"Wasn't there somebody she could call?" I asked, horrified at the thought of the lonely vigil. "Weren't there neighbors?"

"They didn't have a phone," Mother reminded me, "and there were no neighbors for miles. That was the reason Ryan moved to the mountains, to be away from distractions. No, Julia just sat there all night long, becoming more and more frightened, and the next morning when the sun came up she started walking to the village.

"She said she had walked about five miles when she saw a car coming up the road, and it was the sheriff from Pine Crest. The wreck had been discovered. Some fishermen had been following the creek back through the valley and had come upon it and looked up and seen the passage it had traveled from the top of the ledge."

"Then that's why you weren't notified sooner."

"Yes. By the time they took Julia to identify the car and then back to the house to find our address, it was afternoon. The sheriff drove back to Pine Crest to send the telegram. He wanted Julia to go with him or at least to call in some of the women from the village to stay with her, but she refused to see anybody. She just stayed alone in the house and waited for us to come."

"Poor thing," I breathed.

"Seventeen is such a vulnerable age," Mother said. "The adjustment will be hard. She doesn't even know us. I hope so much we can make her happy here."

"We will," I said. "Albuquerque's a nice place to live."

"But to make a whole new life, to start from scratch among people who must seem like strangers! How lost she must feel! I'm afraid much of the responsibility will fall upon you, dear. You're the one closest to her age, the one she'll be best able to relate to."

"Don't worry," I said. "I'll take care of her. I'll introduce her to my friends and take her to the pool and—oh, everything. It'll be all right, Mother."

"I surely hope so."

There were footsteps on the stairs and my father's voice called, "Leslie?"

"In here, dear," Mother called back, forcing a little smile as he appeared in the doorway. "Did you get Julia installed in Rae's room?"

"Well, she's up there if that's what you mean," Dad said. "I didn't know where to tell her to put things. As usual, the place looks like a cyclone hit it."

"I was going to get it straightened," I said hurriedly. "I didn't know you were coming home so soon. I'll go up now and clear out some drawers in the bureau."

"We'll get a second one," Mother said, "as soon as possible. Take up some hangers."

"Okay," I said.

I went to Bobby's room for the hangers because they seem to breed in his closet, and carried them upstairs and paused before the closed door of my room. I wondered if I should knock. I decided I should and rapped softly, and immediately Julia's voice said, "Yes?"

"It's Rae," I said. "I've got some hangers for your clothes."

"Come in."

I opened the door. Julia was not lying down, as I had expected, but was seated on the edge of one of the twin beds, looking about her. Automatically I found myself following her gaze, seeing the room as through the eyes of a stranger—the pale yellow walls, the gay posters, the crowded bookshelf, the cluttered bureau top, the pile of clothing tossed on the wicker chair.

"It's kind of messy," I said.

"That's all right."

"I'm not very neat. I'll try to be better now that you're here."

I went over to the chair and picked up the clothes. It wasn't that much, really, just my pajamas and the shirt I had worn the day before and my tennis shoes. I crammed them into the top drawer of the bureau and then stood wondering which drawers I should empty and what I should do with the stuff.

"Mother says we'll be getting another bureau."

"I didn't bring a heap of things," Julia said. "I won't need much room for 'em."

"Then I'll give you the two drawers at the bottom. That is, unless you want the top ones."

"I don't care." Julia was still gazing about her, those strange eyes moving in a slow, careful path, missing nothing. "Who's the boy in the picture?"

"Mike Gallagher," I said. "He lives next door."

"Is he your solid feller?"

"My boyfriend, you mean? No—yes—I guess you could call him that. I don't wear his ring or anything."

"He's good looking."

"Yes," I agreed with a touch of pride. Mike *was* good looking with his broad shoulders and easy grin and that mop of blond hair. "You'll be meeting him tonight. We have a movie date. At least, we did have." It occurred to me that it was not the politest thing in the world to take off with a date on the first night Julia was with us. "Maybe you'd like to go. It's the early feature, and we'd planned on taking Bobby."

"No, thank you." Julia turned to look at me directly for the first time. It was the same way in which she had looked at the room, with a deep, penetrating gaze that took in every detail as though making a mental photograph that would be stored forever in the files of memory. Those eyes bored into me with such intensity that they gave me a feeling of having been caught and pinned in place by a physical force. I could almost feel their progress past the light skin and the sprinkling of freckles, through the hard bones of the skull, into the absolute core of my being. It was a strange feeling being studied so intently. I shifted uncomfortably and turned my own eyes away.

"How do your folks feel about having me here?" Julia asked.

"They want you," I said. "They want you very much. Almost the first thing Mother said after the telegram came was 'We'll have to go get Julia.'"

"And your father?"

"Dad too, of course. He wants whatever Mother wants, always."

"They get along well then, your folks?"

"Well, sure. They married each other, didn't they?" It was such a strange question I wondered if I had misunderstood it. Some of the terms Julia used and the way she pronounced her words were disconcerting. Perhaps, I thought, she had meant something entirely different.

But my answer seemed to satisfy her. I felt those eyes draw out of me, and she settled back on the bed.

"Tell me about your family," she said. "What are they like? I want to know all about them."

It was my bed she was lying on. I wondered if I should tell her and then I thought, no, it doesn't matter. I could take the other bed for one night. Preferring one bed over the other was simply a matter of habit.

"You must be tired," I said. "I'll leave you alone for a while so you can get a nap."

"No, don't. Stay and talk to me." It was more a command than a request. "If I'm going to live here I need to know about everybody. Tell me about your brothers. Which one is the oldest?"

"Peter," I said. "He's eighteen, and he'll be going to the University in the fall. He's the musical one in the family. He plays clarinet and alto sax with a combo and in the daytime he works in a music store. Bobby's eleven and likes to play baseball." I paused. "Didn't Aunt Marge ever talk about us? Didn't you see the picture Mother sent at Christmas?"

"I must have," Julia said, "but I don't remember it. What about you? Do you go away to school like I do?"

"No," I said. "I go to Highland High, right here in Albuquerque. This summer I'm not doing anything much, at least, not yet. I applied for jobs a lot of places, but so far nobody's called me. I babysit for people and I help Mother in the darkroom, and I cook dinners and things when she's got a job to get out. She does illustrations for magazines, you know."

"And your father? Where does he work?"

"He's an engineer and works for the government. That's how we get to belong to the Coronado Club out on the base and use their pool and go to the dances. They have a lot of things going on out there for teenagers. I'll take you to some of them when—well, when you're ready. I know it'll be a while before you'll feel like doing things."

I tried to picture Julia at the pool, laughing and splashing and joking around with Carolyn and me. It was a hard thing to imagine. It was equally hard to picture her at a dance. Those huge eyes gazing up at me from the pillow, the thin face half lost in the flood of raven hair, seemed to belong to someone from another world.

The words on Aunt Marge's card came back to me—"Our angel Julie is home for the holidays and the house is filled with singing." "Julie" was such a carefree nickname, it did not seem possible that it could ever have been used for Julia.

"Julia," I said haltingly, knowing that I must say something, but what? How could I reach through the wall of grief that separated us and give comfort? Julia's attempt at making small talk was touching, but I knew the effort it must be taking.

"Julia," I said again helplessly, and was interrupted by the sound of scratching at the door. Relief swept over me. Here was the diversion we needed!

"There's somebody here to see you," I said. "Another member of the family." I went to the door and opened it. "Come in, Trickle. I want you to meet a new friend."

"Who is it?" Julia asked, pulling herself to a sitting position. Her voice went strangely flat. "Oh. It's a dog."

"Don't call him that," I said. "You'll hurt his feelings. He thinks he's people. He won't even eat dogfood because he thinks he ought to eat the same things we do. Mother and Dad gave him to me on my twelfth birthday."

Julia's body seemed to stiffen. "I'm not very good with dogs. They don't like me."

"Trickle will," I told her. "He loves everybody, even the garbage men. Other dogs all bark at the garbage truck, but Trickle just wags his tail."

"Keep him away from me," Julia said. "I mean it, Rachel."

"You can't be afraid of Trickle!" I exclaimed incredulously. "Why, he wouldn't hurt anybody! He's the sweetest natured dog in the world. There's this man who breeds wirehairs up in Santa Fe—his kennel is where my folks got Trickle—and he said that he'd never sold a puppy who was as—"

"Get him out'er here!" Julia said. Her voice slashed through the room as sharp as a whip.

"All right," I said, startled. "Of course, if you're really frightened. But you'll feel differently when you get to know him. You'll love him, I promise."

Then I heard another sound, low and gravelly. It was something I had never once heard in the entire three and eleven-twelfths years that Trickle had been with us. In amazement I turned and stared at my dog. His head was lowered and his ears were back and his lips were drawn away from his teeth. He was growling.

When I think back I realize that this was the moment I received my first hint that something was terribly wrong.

Four

At the time I realized nothing. How could I?

"Trickle, you bad thing!" I said. "What's gotten into you?" And to Julia—"I'm ashamed of him. I've never known him to act like this before."

I took the poor dog by the scruff of the neck and dragged him out into the hall, growling all the way, and then picked him up and carried him down the stairs and put him outside.

"You just stay out," I told him, "until you're in a better mood."

I re-entered the house through the back door and found Peter at the kitchen table, eating a bowl of ice cream and reading *Down Beat*. For a skinny guy, Pete never seemed to stop eating.

As I came in he lifted his head and tossed his hair back out of his eyes and said, "I see the folks got home. Mom was just pulling out of the driveway as I came in."

"Probably headed for the grocery store," I said. "The refrigerator's down to nothing."

"So I discovered." He gestured toward the sink where he had tossed the empty ice cream carton. "Did they bring Julia back with them?"

"Yes. She's up in my room, lying down. I mean, in *our* room," I corrected myself. "Hers and mine."

"What's she like? Is she pretty?"

"No," I said. "In fact, the opposite. Very plain."

"Nice?"

"I guess so. I didn't talk with her very long. She doesn't like dogs."

"Maybe she hasn't been around any."

"That might be it," I acknowledged. "Living at boarding school so much of the time, she wouldn't have had much chance to have pets, would she? Are you rehearsing tonight?"

"Nope," Pete said. "We don't have any engagements coming up till the dance at the club. Why?"

"I've got a date tonight," I said, "but I felt funny about going out and leaving Julia on her first night here. If you're going to be home, you can entertain her."

"Now, wait a minute," Pete said. He laid down his spoon with such force that it clattered against the side of the bowl. "Do you mean you're planning to stick me with making conversation with some homely female cousin all evening while you're sliding out from under? Where are you going anyway?"

"To a show, and we're taking Bobby."

"Well, take her too, then."

"I offered," I said self-righteously, "and she doesn't want to go." I knew what was behind his reaction. Pete pretended he didn't like girls, but in actuality he was painfully shy with them.

"You might as well get to know her," I told him. "After all, she's going to be living here."

Before he could object any further I went on through the swinging door into the den and turned on the television. Pretty soon Bobby came in, smelling like old tennis shoes and chewing gum, which was the way Bobby usually smelled on summer afternoons, and lay down on the floor, and we watched the Lucy show together until Mother got home from the store and it was time to help her fix dinner.

It seemed funny that night to see the table set with six places instead of five and to know that it would be that way every night from then on. Bobby got to the table first, as usual, and was sent back to wash the backsides of his hands. Peter went to bring in an extra chair from the kitchen, and I went upstairs to get Julia.

I rapped and said, "Dinner!" and Julia answered, "All right. I'm coming," so I went back down to the others and we waited.

We waited and waited, and finally Mother put the chops back into the oven to keep them warm and Dad said, "Are you sure she heard you?"

"She answered," I said. "She said she was coming."

"Girls," Bobby grumbled. "They're never on time for anything."

"At least, they wash the backs of their hands," I told him.

"So, you don't eat with the backs of your hands, do you?" Bobby countered.

"It's the backs that the other people at the table have to look at," Dad said, and they went into the usual routine which we all heard at least twice a week. When it was over Julia was still not down and the chops were beginning to smell as though they were burning.

"Maybe I'd better go up and check on her," Mother began. "She could have dozed back off—"

And then she was there, standing in the doorway. Julia.

I knew then why it had taken her so long. Julia had dressed for dinner. The dress she had chosen was pale yellow with a long, swirling skirt and bell sleeves. It was a lovely dress, a strangely familiar dress. I had an immediate feeling that I had seen one like it recently on someone else, someone it had looked really good on.

But it wasn't good on Julia. It seemed to hang wrong with the shoulder seams not quite in the right place so that her wrists extended too far below the end of the sleeves. It was tight across the chest, too, and the color was wrong. Julia was too sallow to wear that pale, butterfly shade of yellow.

But Mother got up and hugged her and said, "Honey, you look lovely," and Dad smiled and said, "It's been a long time since I've had the pleasure of seeing a girl at this table wearing anything but blue jeans. Have you met your cousins, Pete and Bobby?"

The boys grunted greetings, and Julia said something appropriate. Then everybody sat down and Mother went out and got the chops and we had dinner.

What did we talk about at that dinner? I'm trying to remember. Just ordinary things, I guess. Mother had found a letter waiting for her from a

magazine that wanted a picture of young people
playing on sleds. "Didn't we take some last winter?" she mused: "I'll have to check my negative
file. Magazines buy half a year ahead, Julia, so the
calls for winter pictures come in the summer." Dad
remarked on some items in the evening paper.
"Professor Jarvis is certainly staying active in his
retirement. I see where he's giving one of his occult
lectures at the University Women's Club." Bobby
wanted to know if he could get a new grass-catch-
er for the lawn mower.

I contributed the story of Trickle's strange per-
formance.

"I've never heard him growl before," I said. "I
wonder if he's feeling bad or something."

"Maybe he's been eating grass," Bobby suggested. "That makes dogs sick."

"No, it doesn't," I told him. "Dogs eat grass *because* they're sick. It makes them better."

Julia didn't often enter the conversation, but she
listened. Her eyes went from one of us to another,
studying our faces as she took in our words.

It wasn't until Peter dropped his fork that she
spoke up abruptly.

"Somebody's coming."

"What?" Peter said, startled.

"Oh—nothing." Julia looked embarrassed. "It's
just something the hill people say. A pussy superstition."

"How interesting!" Mother exclaimed. "I imagine
you heard about all sorts of fascinating superstitions, living in that area of the Ozarks. Or were you
there long enough to be exposed to them?"

"I heard them from my folks," Julia said. "They

talked about them a lot. My father wanted atmosphere in his book. That's why they hired Sarah from the village. They used her to learn how the jakey folks talked."

"You make it sound like a foreign country," Peter said, interested despite himself.

"It was," Julia said. "Anyway, the parts where we were seemed that way. It's like nothing there has changed in a thousand years. People get born there and live their whole lives there just like their foreparents. Their idea of a trip to the big city is going into Pine Crest on Saturdays. You try to tell them there's a whole big world on the other side of the mountains, and they look at you like you're crazy."

"Your father must have liked it there," Dad inserted gently. "After all, he chose to live there."

"But not forever," Julia said. "Just long enough to write his book. He'd have been done with it by summer. We were coming back then—this very summer, along about August—"

She let the sentence fall away, too painful to continue. We all shifted uncomfortably in a sudden search for a new direction in which to turn the conversation.

I grabbed at an old, reliable subject.

"What did you do on dates? Were there movies or bowling alleys or anything?"

"Nothing," Julia said. "Folks just sat and talked. That was courting. And if a girl wasn't married by eighteen she was an old maid for sure. Sarah was twenty-two, and you should of heard the things people'd say about her—that she was stuck-up and thought she was too good for any local fellows and waiting for a prince to come riding in and carry her off somewhere. After she came to work for us they wouldn't hardly talk to her. Not that she cared, of course."

"Did you have a backwoods boyfriend?" Peter asked her. It was such an unbelievable question to come from Peter that we all turned to him in amazement. He avoided our eyes, keeping his trained on Julia.

"No. Not really."

"Not really? Or not *any?*"

"The boys there weren't my type," Julia said. "When I pick somebody he'll be ambitious. A college man, maybe."

She raised her eyes to meet his, and a deep flush began to rise in Peter's face. He dropped his own gaze to his plate and began fumbling around trying to put butter on a slice of bread he had already buttered.

"Can I have some more potatoes?" Bobby asked.

"How did the car run while we were away?" Dad asked Peter. "Were you still getting that chirping sound in the engine?"

The conversation was channeled off into other directions, and Julia slipped from it as easily as she had entered. When I look back I think that was the only real talking she did throughout the meal.

Bobby and I were clearing the table when the doorbell rang.

"That will be Mike," I said. "We're going to an early movie. Do you want to come with us, Bob? I forgot to ask earlier."

"Are you kidding?" Bobby asked incredulously. "With 'Kung Fu' on television?"

"I hope you're not planning to go out in those

blue jeans," Mother said. "They have holes in the knees."

"They're my favorite jeans!" I protested. "I've just got them broken in!"

The bell rang again and I went to answer it. I let Mike in and went up to change clothes, because even though I was in the right and the jeans were perfectly appropriate for movie going, it wasn't worth the hassle of making an issue of the fact.

When I reached my room I saw Julia had started to unpack. Her suitcase stood open and the contents had been shoved about as though she had hurriedly dug through her things in order to locate the yellow dress. As I passed the case my foot struck something and sent it rolling across the floor. I bent to pick it up and discovered it was a small jar that looked as though it might contain some sort of cosmetic, although it did not have a label.

Curious, I unscrewed the top and saw that it held some sort of yellowish powder. It had an odd smell and I capped it again quickly, deciding then and there that one thing I wouldn't do with Julia was borrow her makeup. I stuck the jar back into the case, from which it had evidently fallen, and continued across the room to the closet.

When I went back downstairs Mike was sitting in the living room with the family, telling them about a job he had just been offered as lifeguard at the Coronado Club pool.

"I had my name on the list since last fall," he said, "but I never expected to get it, not with every other guy in town applying. But this afternoon they called and said it's mine if I want it. *If I want it*—wow! The perfect summer job!"

"What about your lawn jobs?" I asked him. "Aren't you supposed to be doing Professor Jarvis's yard every week?"

"I'll pass that to Bobby. The professor doesn't care who does it as long as it gets done." He got to his feet. "We'd better get going or we'll miss the start. It's good to have you folks home again. It was nice meeting you, Julia. I live next door so you'll have to get used to having me around."

"Thank you," Julia said politely, and Mike and I left.

"Well, what did you think of her?" I asked when we were in the car.

"I didn't think anything. I hardly saw her." Mike turned the key in the ignition. "What do *you* think?"

"She's not what I expected," I said. "She's sort of strange. She has an odd way of talking—when she talks. Which isn't much. She uses funny words —'pussy' and 'jakey' and things like that. Slang, I guess, but not like the kind we use around here."

"What did you expect?" Mike asked. "She's from another part of the country. She probably thinks we're the ones who talk funny."

"But she only spent summers in the Ozarks," I said. "She went to school in New England. And it's not just her accent and the odd terms. She has a way of pausing before she speaks as though she's afraid she's not going to say the right thing. She seems so tense and—well, almost *afraid* of us."

"Probably shy," Mike said. "Who wouldn't be, moving into a house with a nut like you in it?"

"I'd have to be a nut to date *you*!" I said, reaching over to ruff up his hair.

And so we kept on jabbing at each other and kidding around, the way we always did when we were together, and it wasn't long before we had both forgotten about Julia completely.

The movie was a good one. We ran into Carolyn there with her boyfriend Rick, and we all went out afterward to Frank's Drive-In and had cokes and french fries, so it was eleven-thirty or so by the time we pulled up in front of the house and parked to say goodnight.

The house was dark, and when Mike switched off his headlights everything was black for a few minutes. Then slowly things became visible once more—the maple tree in the front yard, the brick planter, Bobby's bike leaning against the side of the garage. The curve of the half-moon looked as though it were caught in the branches of the maple, and the sweet breath of early summer came softly through the open windows, and Mike put his arm around me and pulled me over and kissed me.

"Why didn't we start doing this sooner?" he whispered.

"At the movie?"

"No, you nut. Last year. Or the year before. How long did we know each other before I ever got around to kissing you?"

"I'll figure it up sometime," I said. "After all, we've known each other since we were on tricycles. You never even used to notice me except to tease me about my freckles."

"Well, there wasn't that much to notice," Mike said. "Let's face it, there've been some changes in the past year, all in the right places."

"You're awful!" I exclaimed, not meaning it at

all. I lifted my face so he could kiss me again, and he was just about to when there was a squeak and a click from the direction of the house. We both stiffened and the moment was gone.

"That was the screen door," Mike said. "Was somebody sitting out on your porch?"

"I can't imagine who," I said. "It's too late for my folks to be up and all the lights are off inside."

We got out of the car and walked together across the yard, Mike with his arm around my shoulders, and as we approached the porch we saw that there was indeed someone there. It was Peter.

"Hi," he said. "How was the show?"

"Pretty good," Mike said. "Did you have a rehearsal tonight?"

"Nope. Stayed home."

"What are you doing out here?" I asked. "Waiting for us?"

"Why would I do that?"

"Then what?"

"Enjoying the moonlight. Is there any rule that says a guy can't sit on his own porch?"

"None at all."

I could not see his face in the shadows, but there was something strange about his voice. Pete usually had a sort of deadpan voice, the kind that can tell jokes, and you don't even know they're jokes until you think about them for a while. But tonight there was a different note, a sort of lift.

"Have you been out here long?" I asked.

"Not too long. Why?"

"We thought we heard the screen door close."

"That was Julia," Pete said. "She went inside as you drove up."

"She was out here with you?"

"Well, sure. How else could she go inside?" He sounded defensive. "What is this anyway, a third degree?"

"Hey, you two, cut the squabbling," Mike said. "Somebody might think you were brother and sister." He tightened his arm around my shoulders in what would have been a hug if Pete hadn't been there. "See you tomorrow, Carrot-top."

"Good night, Mike," I said, wishing Pete would go in ahead of me. But he didn't, so Mike went striding off across the lawn to his own house. The moonlight tumbled into his hair as he came out on the far side of the shadow of the maple tree, making it look like a tangle of silver.

He turned once and waved back at us and crossed on into his own yard. I went up the steps and across the porch and put my hand out for the door. I realized suddenly that Peter was not coming behind me.

I stopped and turned back. He was still sitting there on the porch swing, gazing out at the moon in the tree branches.

"Hey, Peter," I said. "Aren't you coming in?"

"In a few minutes," he said. "It's nice out here. I want to sit and think a while."

That tone was back in his voice again, soft and happy. I stood there wondering, and then thought, well, let him sit if he wants to. What's the difference?

So I said, "Good night."

"Good night," Pete said, and then, just as I was going inside, he said, "Rae, you were wrong."

"Wrong?"

"Dead wrong. In fact, crazy." He didn't turn his head. "You said she wasn't pretty."

"You think she is?" I asked in surprise.

"She's more than pretty," Peter said softly. "She's beautiful."

Five_____

What happened that night out there in the moonlight between Peter and Julia, I was never to
know. Peter did not tell me, and when I reached
my room upstairs I found the lights out. In the thin
stream of moonlight from the open window I could
see a dark form stretched out on my bed.

"Julia?" I said softly.

There was no answer.

It seemed impossible that she could have gone
to bed and fallen asleep so quickly. Still, I thought,
she had certainly had a long and emotionally exhausting day. I was tempted to turn on the light in
order to look at her again. Peter had called her
"beautiful"—Peter, who had never called a girl
beautiful before—and I wanted to see why.

But people just don't turn on lights in rooms
where someone else is sleeping, or pretending to
sleep, and so I undressed in the dark, groping
through two different bureau drawers for my pajamas because I couldn't remember how I had ar-

ranged things, and crawled into the other twin
bed.

I'll look at her in the morning, I told myself.

The thought must have stayed with me through
the night, because the moment I wakened I turned
over to stare at the girl in the opposite bed, and I
saw at once that something had changed.

Julia was already awake, lying on her back with
her hands under her head, gazing at the ceiling.
Her thick, black hair was spread out across the
pillow like a frame for the thin, high boned face.
The thing that was different was the expression.
No longer did she have the nervous, half frightened look of the day before. Her face was relaxed
and her lips were curved in a slight smile.

"Rachel," she said without turning her head,
"will you go with me today to buy some clothes?"

I jumped at the sound of her voice. "How did
you know I was awake?" I asked her.

"I felt your eyes open." She turned then, stretch-
ing lazily like a cat and lifting herself up on one
elbow so that she faced me. Her eyes seemed lighter than the day before, softer, less penetrating.
"Will you?"

"Sure," I said. I had no plans for the day. "What
sort of clothes do you want to shop for?"

"Jeans like yours. With the wide bottoms. What
do you call them?"

"Flares?"

"Yes, flares. And some shirts like the one you
had on yesterday when we got here. And—oh, a
lot of things. I need almost everything."

"How come?" I asked. "Did you wear uniforms
at your school?"

Julia hesitated and then nodded. "Yes, that's

right. I didn't even bother to bring them with me. I want to dress the way you do, to wear the kinds of things that you wear here."

"Okay," I said. "We'll get you fixed up so you'll look like a member of the gaggle."

"Of what?"

"The gaggle—that's what Mike calls my friend Carolyn and me when we get together. It's sort of a joke because he says we chatter so much."

"Oh." She didn't laugh, but the little half smile remained on her lips. "Mike seems nice."

"He is," I said. "He kids around a lot, but he's a great guy."

"He's very good looking."

"I think so too." I thought, this is the time to ask her about last night and Peter, but I couldn't seem to make myself do it. So instead I said, "We'd better get up. I smell bacon cooking," and got out of bed.

The work day at the Laboratories was pushed ahead an hour in the summertime, so Dad had already left for work by the time we reached the kitchen. Mother was sitting at the table, drinking her coffee and reading "Dear Abby," and Pete and Bobby were both stuffing down eggs and bacon.

"Morning," I said, and Mother looked up from the paper and smiled and said, "Good morning, girls. Did you sleep well?" and Peter flushed pink under his freckles and said, "Hi, there," not looking at me but at Julia.

"We're going shopping today," I said. "Julia wants to get some summer clothes."

"That's a good idea," Mother said. "In fact, I was going to suggest it myself. The things girls wear at boarding school are sure to be different from what they wear around a place like Albuquerque. I'd go with you, except that I have to print up those snow scenes and get them into the mail."

"I think I'll call Carolyn," I said. "She loves to go shopping, and it will be a chance for Julia to meet her. Maybe Mrs. Baker will run us over to Winrock."

"I'll drive you over," Peter offered. "I can get to work a couple of minutes late without hurting anything."

It was so out of character for Peter that both Mother and I turned to him with our mouths hanging open, and Bobby nearly dropped his toast.

"Boy!" he exclaimed. "Now I've heard everything! Pete Bryant offering to take a bunch of girls shopping and nobody even asked him!"

"Cut it out," Pete said, looking embarrassed. "The shopping center's right on my way to work."

"I'll give you the credit cards," Mother said. "For heaven's sake, don't lose them."

So I called Carolyn, who wanted to come, of course, as she was dying to get a look at Julia. We stopped at her house to pick her up, and then Peter drove us to Winrock and dropped us off there, and Carolyn and I took Julia through the stores. I had a few qualms at first about how Carolyn and Julia would get along together. Julia was so different from all of our school friends that I still felt sort of awkward with her myself. But I needn't have worried. She seemed to take to Carolyn immediately and though she didn't talk much she smiled a lot, and she listened to all of Carolyn's and my suggestions as we swept her along from store to store.

"What about House of Fabrics?" I suggested

after we had bought jeans and two pullover shirts and an India print blouse. "Mother says there's a sale there. I want to make a dress to wear to the teen night dance on the fifteenth."

"That's a great idea," Carolyn said enthusiastically. "Rick's seen everything I own at least a hundred times. I'd like to surprise him for once and show up in something different."

So we went to House of Fabrics and picked out patterns and material. Carolyn got a pale blue with a white design going through it and I went wild and got pink. "At least, I can be sure no other redhead will be wearing it," I said, laughing. "Julia, what are you choosing?"

"I don't sew," Julia said. "Besides, I don't need a dress. I have my yellow."

"Yes," I said, "but still—" I struggled to think of a way to say politely that although the dress was lovely, it was not a dress that was becoming to Julia. It belonged on someone else, someone with lighter hair and complexion—someone—but who? The question of the night before leapt back into my mind, tugging at the edges of my memory in irritating little jerks. Where in the world was it that I had seen a dress like Julia's, and who was it who was wearing it?

"Do you have a swimming suit, Julia?" Carolyn asked, unaware of my mental conflict. "If not, you'll really need one. We all spend a lot of time at the pool out at the club."

So we went back to Penney's where we had purchased the shirts and took a look at the bikinis.

Julia picked out a couple and went into the dressing room to try them on.

"What do you think of my cousin?" I asked Carolyn as we waited.

"I like her," she said immediately. "She's sort of exotic, isn't she, with those big dark eyes? And she has such an interesting way of talking, as though she's always looking for just the right word to express her meaning. I love the way she says 'yeller' —like a hillbilly, one minute—and sounds just as refined as anybody the next. She's just a doll!"

"Peter has a crush on her," I confided.

"You're kidding! *Peter?*" Carolyn widened her eyes incredulously. "Old woman-hating Peter with a crush! Say, do you suppose he'd want to take her to the dance? We could triple."

"I think his band is playing for the dance," I said. "But we could take Julia and he could join us afterward. I don't know how he'd feel about that or whether Julia likes dances or if she'd want to go out anywhere so soon after a family tragedy. But I can ask them and—"

I let the sentence drop because Julia was sticking her head out from behind the curtain of the dressing room.

"Come see what you think," she called.

Carolyn and I went over, and Julia pulled back the curtain a little way so we could see her in the suit. I think I made some sort of gasping sound. It wasn't polite, I knew, but I was so stunned I couldn't help it, for in that swimming suit Julia was —well—incredible.

Although all of us teenagers wore bikinis, it was seldom that you ever saw anybody built exactly right for one. By the time a girl got enough up top to fill one out properly she usually had too much

down below. Julia was the exception. She didn't
look like a girl, but like a young woman. Now I
could understand why the bodice of the yellow
dress had looked so tight, for she had the kind of
figure I had always dreamed of having someday,
maybe when I was about twenty. Her waist was
small and her stomach absolutely flat and she
curved softly in all the right places, and her legs
were long and slim but full enough through the
calves so no one would ever call them skinny.

"Wow!" Carolyn expressed it for both of us.
"You look just great! That's your suit, all right!"

"Do you think the color's right?" Julia asked,
frowning a little.

"Perfect," I said, although until then I hadn't
even noticed the color. It was a light pink of almost the same shade as the material I had chosen
for my new dress. With it for contrast, Julia's skin
no longer appeared sallow but creamy and rich
looking.

"It's lovely," I said. "It couldn't be better, Julia,
really!"

I paid for the suit with Mother's credit card and
we stopped at Walgreen's for cokes and then we
caught the bus for home. We all three crammed
into one seat, and Carolyn started telling us about
her adventures wall-cleaning. Carolyn is made
for story telling; she has one of those rubber
faces that can go into a hundred different expres-
sions, and by the time she was halfway through I
was laughing so hard I was crying.

Julia was laughing too. I had not seen her laugh
before. She was a little stiff about it, as though she
wasn't used to laughing much, or as if she didn't

quite know why the story was funny but wanted to be part of things anyway.

Carolyn must have seen this, because when we got off the bus at the corner of our block she slipped her arm through Julia's and fell into step beside her as though they had been friends for a long time. It was a kind thing to do, and I felt pleased that she liked my cousin and was making such an effort to be nice to her. At the same time I felt sort of funny, walking behind them, because the sidewalk wasn't wide enough for three unless somebody walked in the gutter.

It was one o'clock by this time, and the sun was high and pleasantly warm, although not hot the way it would be in a couple of weeks. In the yard before the Gallaghers', Professor Jarvis was kneeling in the grass, putting in a line of petunias along the edge of the driveway. The professor was retired now, but until two years ago he had taught with the sociology department at the University of New Mexico.

As we came abreast, he looked up and smiled and raised a grubby hand by way of greeting. We stopped, and I introduced Julia.

"She's my cousin, Julia Grant," I told him, "from Pine Crest, Missouri. She's living with us now."

"Pine Crest?" The professor nodded appreciatively. "That's in the heart of the Ozarks, isn't it? An interesting area, the bed of a lot of intriguing folklore."

"I'm not really *from* there," Julia said. "I mean, it was my parents who lived there. I was away at school most of the time."

"My uncle was a writer," I said. "He moved to

the mountains to write a novel. He and my aunt were killed in a car wreck last week."

"How sad," the professor said. And to Julia, "I'm so sorry, my dear. I wish your move to Albuquerque were under happier circumstances."

"Thank you," Julia said. "I—I wish so too." It was apparent that the conversation made her uncomfortable. She gave Carolyn's arm a little tug, as though to urge her forward. "It was nice meeting you."

"You feel free to drop over," Professor Jarvis said kindly. "I enjoy chatting with young people. I spent most of my life teaching them and I miss the contact. When you lose touch with youth, you grow old fast."

"You'll never be old," I told him fondly and meant it. The face beneath the thatch of white hair was as bright with life as the flowers he was planting. As Carolyn and Julia moved onward I hung back to watch him place the last of the plants carefully into the trench he had prepared for it and smooth the earth gently over its roots.

"What's Peter doing these days?" he asked me. "He graduated, didn't he? I hope he's planning on college."

"He is," I said. "He's planning to major in music. You know Peter; what other direction would he go?"

We chatted a few minutes about colleges—and summertime—and the growing habits of petunias. Then the professor got to his feet and gathered up the cartons the plants had come in and carried them into the garage, and I strolled on past the Gallaghers' toward my own house.

I was just turning into the front yard when I

heard it—a low rumbling sound, followed by a yelp and a stifled shriek. Then a woman's voice rose in a cry of rage:

"You vigrous, rat-fanged varmant! I'll warp you good for that!"

It was a moment before I realized that the words had come from Julia.

"What on earth!" I exclaimed and broke into a run across the lawn to the porch steps. Julia was down on one knee, her hands clasped tightly around her left ankle. Carolyn was bent over her, and when she straightened and turned to me her face was white with shock.

"What got into him? I've never seen him do a thing like that!"

"What is it?" I demanded. "What happened?"

"It's that dawg of yourn!" Julia cried in a voice so choked with anger that it was all I could do to understand the words. "He flang hisself out and bit me!"

"Trickle bit you?" I couldn't believe what I was hearing. "He couldn't have! I don't believe it!"

"Take a gander at thet and see if you believe it or not!" Julia lifted her hands, and I caught my breath as I saw the blood gushing from the deep tooth marks in the flesh just above the anklebone.

"He was lying on the porch," Carolyn told me shakily, "over there in that patch of sunlight. We started up the steps and he began to wag his tail like he always does. Then suddenly he growled—I've never heard Trickle growl in all the time I've known him! He got up and stood there all stiff with his ears back against his head, and the next moment he jumped right at Julia and bit her! Then he ran off around the side of the house, headed for the back."

"I don't believe it," I said again. But this was not true. Into my mind leapt the picture of Trickle as he had been the night before, his head lowered, his teeth bared. He had growled at Julia then, a low, menacing growl of pure hatred. Was it any more incredible that he had bitten her now?

"Take her into the house," I told Carolyn, "and tell Mother what happened. She'll know how to treat the bite and stop the bleeding. I'm going to find Trickle."

I left the girls there on the steps and went around to the backyard to look in the hollow behind the hydrangea bush. It was the place Trickle always ran when he knew he had done something wrong and was going to be scolded. But he wasn't there.

I searched the yard and went up and down the street calling him, but he didn't come.

Six

Julia sat in silence while Mother cleansed her wound and bandaged it. Then she went upstairs to our room and closed the door.

"She's upset, and no wonder," Mother said. "What an awful thing to have happen on her second day here! Thank goodness I took that dog for his rabies shot only a couple of months ago. What on earth could be wrong with him?"

"I don't know," I said miserably. "I guess he just hates Julia."

"But dogs don't do that," Carolyn said. "Just take a hatred to someone, I mean, without any reason. Could she have mistreated him somehow?"

"She only arrived yesterday," I said. "And it was like this the first time they saw each other. There's just something about her that Trickle doesn't like and he's reacting to it."

"Well, he had better stop reacting," Mother said shortly. "A dog that turns vicious does not belong in a home like ours."

"You don't mean you'd—you'd get rid of him!"
I exclaimed in horror. "Trickle's mine! He's one of
the family!"

"It would break my heart," Mother said. "He *is*
like one of the family. But he's a dog, and if we
have to make a choice between a dog and people,
people come first. My sister's only child means a
great deal more to me than any animal, even
Trickle. So let's just hope nothing like this occurs
again."

There was an awkward silence while we all stood
around and looked at each other. Then Carolyn
said tentatively, "Well, I guess I'd better be going.
I've got some stuff to do at home and some books
to take to the library and things like that."

She didn't really, I could tell. She was uncomfortable with the friction between Mother and me,
and I could not blame her.

"Why don't we get together tonight?" I suggested. "I could come over to your house and we
could play records or something."

"All right," Carolyn started to say, but Mother
broke in before she could form the words.

"Rachel, this is only Julia's second day here."

"I know," I said, "but—"

"You were gone all yesterday evening. I think
tonight it would be very nice if you stayed home
and spent some time making your cousin feel wel-
come."

"Okay," I said. "Okay, okay, okay."

"Rae, I don't like that tone of voice."

"I've got to be going," Carolyn said hurriedly.
"I've just got tons to do, really. Tell Julia good-bye
for me. I really enjoyed meeting her."

"Thank you, Carolyn," Mother said. "I'll tell her."

The day that had begun so pleasantly seemed somehow to have fallen apart. I walked my friend to the door and watched her start off down the street and came back inside.

Mother had vanished. I opened the door that led from the kitchen into the garage and heard the clinking of bottles coming from the storeroom which Dad had converted for her into a darkroom. I knew she was mixing chemicals and was probably going to start an afternoon of printing. Any other time I would have rapped on the door and asked if I could join her; I enjoyed helping her in the darkroom.

At the moment, however, it was the last thing I wanted to do. I'd had enough of being lectured without deliberately letting myself in for another siege of it. I was sure that whatever I did would be wrong, and Mother would jump all over me, and I'd snap back at her.

The afternoon loomed long and empty with nothing to fill it. I wished now I had started earlier to look for a summer job so that I might have had a real chance of finding one. The places where I had left my name had all been discouraging; when they hired summer help it was usually students from the University. I would have liked to have gone to the pool, but there was no way to get there. I would have enjoyed playing records, but the stereo was upstairs in the bedroom which now was half Julia's. She had gone into it and shut the door, and there was no way I could feel at ease with the idea of bursting in upon her.

I didn't realize it at the time, but this was to be the first of many such afternoons during that long, strange summer.

I wound up at last in the backyard with a couple of Dad's old issues of *National Geographic*. I leafed through them idly, looking at the pictures and pausing occasionally to read the captions. In one of them there was an article on Africa. It was illustrated by a photograph of a witch doctor involved in some sort of native ceremony. His face and body were painted in brilliant colors, his arms were raised, and his eyes were glaring straight at the camera.

The impact of those eyes was extraordinary, even in a picture. They seemed to exert a force so powerful that it could not be confined by the printed page. Was this, I wondered, the kind of thing Professor Jarvis gave his lectures about? Did people like this really perform magic?

The caption beneath the picture said that this man was practicing macumba, a form of sorcery which permitted its practitioners to kill at a distance with the concentrated power of their thoughts.

Ridiculous, I told myself, but could not help giving a little shudder as I turned the page.

I finished that magazine and laid it aside and picked up the other. The sun moved slowly down the curve of the sky and the shadow of the elm tree crept toward me until at last the leaf patterns sprinkled themselves across my lap. Eventually it was time to go in and scrub the potatoes and put them in the oven, and while I was doing that Bobby came in with a lump on his head from having been hit with a softball.

"That's a dumb name for it," he told me. "There's nothing soft about it."

I helped him put ice on his forehead to diminish the swelling, and then Mother came in from the darkroom carrying her prints. She spread them out on the kitchen table to evaluate them, and while that was going on Dad got home from work, and Peter soon after him, and things seemed normal again.

Normal—and yet, not quite.

Julia came down to dinner dressed in a pair of her new jeans and the Indian blouse. Her face was pale, and she looked tired and drained of energy. Everyone pounced upon her as though she had been gone for years, and Peter even went so far as to pull out her chair.

"How are you, dear?" Mother asked anxiously. "Is your ankle feeling better?"

"Her ankle?" Dad said. "What happened to her ankle?"

"It was an unbelievable thing," Mother said, and told him what had occurred that morning. Dad's face darkened as he listened, and Peter looked so angry that I was afraid he was going to get up and go looking for Trickle that very moment.

"Wait till I get my hands on that dog," he said grimly. "I'll teach him to go around biting people. Where is he, anyway?"

"I don't know," I said. "He's gone." I felt very much like crying.

"When he comes back," Dad said, "I don't want him in this house. We're not going to risk this sort of thing happening again."

"Not come in the house!" I exclaimed. "But he lives in this house! It's his home!"

"It's summer," Dad said. "It's beautiful weather. He can stay outside. And I don't want him running loose either. One episode of this kind is enough."

"You mean I'll have to tie him?" I asked. The thought of poor Trickle staked out in the yard like a fierce beast was so absurd that I wanted to laugh, and I knew that if I started laughing I would never be able to stop. I could feel the laughter building up inside me, mixing with the tears. "I can't tie him, I just can't! He'd hate it so!"

"Not as much as he'll hate what I'm going to do with him if he so much as growls at Julia another time." It was Peter who said this, squaring his skinny shoulders and sticking out his jaw in a determined fashion as though he were offering to fight a lion single-handed to protect his beautiful lady. It was all so ridiculous and at the same time so awful. I looked up and down the table at the faces of my family, the people I loved most in the world, and except for Bobby who was too busy wrestling with the catsup bottle to take part in the conversation, they were regarding me as coldly as though I were an unpleasant stranger.

"I don't want any more argument," Dad said. "Either Trickle stays outside or we get rid of him altogether. An animal who begins to be—"

He was interrupted by the doorbell. Bobby got up to answer it and came back in with Mike.

"Hi," he said. "I didn't mean to break in on dinner. I'll come back later." It was like a burst of sunshine into a gloom-filled room, and we all relaxed a little.

"Don't be silly," Mother told him. "We're always

glad to see you. Have you eaten yet? There's plenty if you'd like to join us."

"No, thanks. Mom's got things cooking at our house. I just ran over for a minute."

Mike straddled the arm of the sofa and perched there, a little higher than the rest of us, looking down into all of our plates. Glancing up at him, I thought how handsome he was with his face already beginning to pick up its summer tan and his hair fluffed out in a sort of halo around his head from the day spent in the sun and water.

He grinned at me and winked in way of private greeting, and I felt better than I had all afternoon.

"How was work?" I asked. "Do you think you're going to like it?"

"Great. Fantastic. Nothing to do but sit on my tower and watch the pretty girls in their new swimming suits."

"I got a suit today," Julia said. "Rae and Carolyn helped me pick it out. It's awfully pretty."

"Really? How nice." Mother smiled across at her. "In all the excitement over the Trickle attack I never did get around to asking about the morning's shopping. That's a new blouse you're wearing, isn't it? Did you find some other things?"

"These jeans are new too," Julia said, "and I bought some tops. Thank you so much for letting me get them. I hope we didn't spend too much."

"I'm sure you didn't," Dad said. "The important thing is that you got some things you'll enjoy wearing. I guess styles vary in different parts of the country. You'll feel more comfortable living here if you're dressed like the rest of the girls."

Picturing Julia in her new swimming suit, I

almost choked. There was no way that Julia in a bikini was ever going to look like the rest of us. Thinking of the suit reminded me of Carolyn's question while we were at Penney's waiting for Julia to emerge from the dressing room, and I asked it now, more out of duty than because I really wanted to.

"Julia, do you think you'd like to go to the dance at the Coronado Club next week? A bunch of us will be going and Peter's going to play."

"Why—I don't know," Julia said hesitantly, "I don't dance very well."

"You don't have to dance," Peter said quickly. "You can just sit at a table and enjoy the music. I can come over and sit with you at intermissions. That's a great idea!"

"I don't know," Julia said again. She glanced across at Mother. "Do you think it would be—all right?"

"I think it would, dear," Mother said gently. "It would be a chance for you to meet Rae's and Peter's friends, people who will be your friends too in the time ahead. I know how you feel, but I'm sure your parents would want you to go out and be with young people as soon as possible. It's a much healthier thing than staying alone and grieving.

"She could come with Rae and me," Mike said. "Then Pete could join us later if he wanted to."

"Sure," Pete said. "And we could all go out some place for something to eat afterward. Come on, Julia—I want you to hear the band. We've worked up some good arrangements."

Julia's glance flickered from Mike's face to Pete's and back to Mike's again.

"You're all so nice to want me," she said. "I—I suppose I should go. It just seems—so soon—"

"It's the way your parents would want it," Dad said firmly and reached over to put his hand on her shoulder. "Life goes on, and we have to go on with it. You're a brave girl, Julia; I can't tell you how proud we are to have you part of our family."

Mike stayed on a few minutes longer and then I excused myself to walk him to the door. I went with him out onto the porch to see him down the steps. It was still dusk, a faded, gentle light, lingering softly as twilight does in summer. The children down the block were all out playing, enjoying the fun of a delayed nightfall. Their voices lifted, light and giggly, punctuated by squeals. Some little girl was chanting the old rope-jumping jingle:

> *Pomp-pomp-pompadour, Janie,*
> *Calling for Ida at the door—*
> *Now Ida is the one who's gonna have the fun,*
> *And we won't need Janie anymore!*

"I remember being ten years old," I said. It seemed suddenly a million years ago.

"I remember too," Mike said. "You were pretty scrawny and your nose ran a lot."

"Liar!" I cried, outraged.

"Okay—okay—I was just kidding." He rumpled my hair. "You've got a cute nose, and I guess it didn't used to run any more than most kids' noses. Want to do something after dinner?"

"What?" I asked.

"Oh, walk over to the park or something. It'll still be light. We could take Trickle on his leash. It would be a good outing for him."

"I don't know where he is," I said. "He ran off somewhere."

"Well, just us then. Or we could take your cousin along if you want to."

"Well—" I paused, searching for words. I didn't know how to say it, but I didn't want to take Julia with us to the park. Taking her with us to the dance was enough. At that moment all I wanted in the world was to be alone with Mike in some far place away from arguments and problems and family obligations, some place where I could be horrid and selfish and not spend one thought on brave, suffering Julia who needed us so.

"I can't," I said. "Mother wants me home. She says going out last night was enough. She and I haven't been getting along too well today."

"You and your mom?" Mike was surprised. "You two always get along!"

"It was just one of those days," I said. "Something happened and—well, it set us off."

"It'll iron out by tomorrow," Mike said comfortingly. "Your mom's pretty cool. Want to come out to the pool in the morning and watch me laboring away on my watch tower?"

"Laboring!" I said, jokingly. "What a cushy job!" But my heart wasn't in the kidding. Mike must have realized it because he leaned over and gave me a quick kiss on the end of the nose before he started down the steps.

He was halfway down the walk and I was re-entering the house when he called back, "Rae, isn't that Trickle?"

"Where?" I cried, turning.

"Over there under the corner of the porch."

"Trickle!" I exclaimed. "Is that you?"

I went down the steps and over to the place where Mike was pointing, and it was indeed Trickle. He had dug a little trench and was lying in it, and when I got close to him he began to lift his tail and let it fall with a slow, even beat to let me know that he was glad to see me.

"He looks funny," I said, dropping to my knees and running my hand over the silly head. "Doesn't he look funny, Mike?"

Mike came over to stand beside me.

"He looks sickish," he said. "Maybe he's eaten something he shouldn't have. You'd better leave him outside tonight. You don't want him upchucking all over the house."

"I don't have much choice," I told him. "Dad says I can't bring him inside anyway. I think I'll take him around to the back and fix up a bed for him to sleep on."

Trickle wouldn't get up when I prodded him, so I picked him up in my arms and carried him around the side of the house to the backyard. I left him there while I went in through the kitchen door and got him a bowl of water and I stopped on the way back to take a cushion off of the lawn chair. I brought them back to him and set them both down on the ground beside him.

Trickle sniffed at the cushion and then gave a great sigh and settled himself in the grass beside it. He didn't even look at the water.

"Don't you worry," I whispered, moving one hand to scratch his tummy. "People aren't going to stay mad at you forever. Everybody has a right to lose his temper once in a while, even a dog. By tomorrow I bet it's all forgotten and you're back inside sleeping on the foot of my bed."

But when tomorrow came, nobody had forgotten anything. Dad sent Bobby out with a rope to tie Trickle to the elm tree.

Seven _____

On Monday of the following week we had the memorial service for Aunt Marge and Uncle Ryan, and on Tuesday the boxes containing their personal possessions arrived from Springfield. Dad and Peter carted them up to the attic and stored them there against the day when Julia might feel like opening them and going through the contents.

"Not now," she said. "I just can't do it now."

Dad said, "Of course not, honey. Nobody expects you to do anything right now except eat and sleep and try to get used to your new family."

They were standing in the hallway outside the door to the den and I was seated on the den floor, cutting out the material for my new dress. Their voices came to me as clearly as though they were in the same room.

"That part isn't hard," Julia said. "You're so good to me, Tom, I'm used to you already."

The scissors slipped from my hand and tumbled soundlessly into a mound of pink cloth. Had that been Julia speaking, my cousin Julia? That throaty voice, rich with warm affection—could it have been the same one that had risen in fury—"You vigrous, rat-fanged varmant!"—a shriek of rage that had shrilled through the front yard?

And—"Tom"! She had called my father "Tom." Why not "Uncle Tom" as she called my mother "Aunt Leslie"? True, it was Mother who had been her mother's sister, but I had called Julia's father "Uncle Ryan" even though he was no blood relation. "Tom" sounded so strange from the lips of a girl so little older than myself, so oddly familiar, almost rude.

But my father did not seem to find it so. He laughed, a pleased little laugh, and I could picture him ruffling her hair, the way he did mine when he was feeling fond and friendly.

"We're not 'being good,' " he said, "we're just 'being family.' We love you, Julie, and we want you to be happy."

Julia went upstairs then and Dad came into the den, looking for the paper. He gave me a playful tap with his foot as he went by and then paused and said, "What's that you're making?"

"A dress," I said, "for the dance. It's the end of this week."

"Pink?" Dad said. "Since when does a carrot-top like you start wearing pink? I thought it was against the law or something."

"Why shouldn't I wear something different once in a while?" I said irritably. "The material was on sale and it's pretty so I bought it."

"Don't get your back up," Dad said, locating the paper and settling himself into a chair to read it. "It's fine with me whatever you wear. You're the one who's always screamed if somebody gave you something pink."

He was right. I had never worn pink. It didn't go with orange hair and freckles. I sat staring down unhappily at the soft piles of rose-colored material. Why I had bought it I simply couldn't imagine. There had been other colors just as pretty that would have looked fine on me. And the pattern—why had I chosen a style so full up top? It was sure to bag, and altering it would take forever. In order to have it in time for the dance, I would have to make the dress according to the pattern, and go looking as though I were wearing somebody's misfitting hand-me-downs.

As it happened, I need not have wasted time worrying. I never wore the pink dress, and I did not go to the dance.

When I woke on Friday morning I knew that something was wrong, but I wasn't sure exactly what it was. I squirmed uncomfortably in my bed, feeling hot and unpleasant and strangely scratchy. I would have liked to have closed my eyes and gone back to sleep, but the morning sunlight reached from the window across the room and fell, light and lemony, upon my face. It was its touch upon my eyelids that had wakened me, and I knew it would not permit me to fall asleep again.

With a sigh I got out of bed and stumbled groggily across the room to the bathroom. I reached for my toothbrush, glanced into the mirror over the basin, and froze. The face that looked back at me was not my own. It was a grotesque mask, bloated and red and ghastly!

For a moment I could not move or speak. I simply stood there staring. Then I gave a strangled gasp and closed my eyes. It couldn't be true, I thought. It was a bad dream, a nightmare, every girl's worst fear come true—to rise in the morning and find that in the night you had changed into some sort of dreadful creature, inhuman and repulsive!

It's the lighting, I told myself frantically, or the mirror or something! I kept my eyes closed a few seconds more and then opened them, and it was not a dream and it was not the lighting. The beady little eyes, peering out from slits in the swollen face, were my eyes, and the curly mass of bright-colored hair that framed the face was also mine.

With a little sob I turned away from the mirror and rushed out of the bathroom.

"What is it?" Julia was sitting up in bed, rubbing the sleep out of her eyes. "Is something the matter?"

"Yes," I choked. "Yes—something is."

"What's wrong?"

"Don't look at me," I said. "I don't want anybody to look at me!"

I opened the bedroom door and ran out into the hall and down the stairs.

"Mother!" I cried. "Mother!"

She was in the kitchen, standing at the stove, with her back to the doorway. As I rushed in she turned and her eyes widened.

"Good Lord," she exclaimed, "what's happened to you?"

"I don't know," I said shakily. "Mother, I'm scared! What could it be?"

"It looks like hives." She shoved the frying pan off the burner and came over to look at me more closely. "Yes, I'd swear it's hives. I had an aunt who used to get them whenever she ate strawberries. The thing is that people who are susceptible to hives usually start getting them in babyhood. I can't imagine having them for the first time as a teenager."

"What can I do about them?" I asked. "How do you get rid of them?"

"I'll call Dr. Morgan," Mother said, "I think he'd better look at you. If it is hives there may be something you can take for them, and if it isn't we want to know what you *do* have. Go get some clothes on and I'll call and see if he'll see you before the regular office hours."

So I went back upstairs to dress and found Julia still in bed, lying on her back, staring at the ceiling. I hurried past her, not speaking, and hauled some clothes out of the bureau and went into the bathroom to dress. There I received another shock, for the ugly red splotches were not confined to my face. I had them all over my body, some of them studded with great white lumps that resembled mosquito bites but were much larger, and my feet were so swollen that I could not wedge them into my shoes.

I stuck my feet into a pair of floppy bedroom slippers and went back down to the kitchen. Bobby was there now, shoveling down cereal, and he let out a low whistle and said, "What's the matter with your face?"

"Mother thinks it's hives," I told him, trying not to cry.

"I talked to the nurse," Mother said. "Dr. Morgan will see you, but they want you to come in the side door so you won't expose the people in the waiting room if this turns out to be something contagious. Come on, I'll drive you over."

An hour later we were home again, assured that I was not contagious. What I had was hives, as Mother had suspected, and Dr. Morgan had prescribed a medication that was to be taken every four hours and told me to take baths with baking soda in the water.

"It's an allergic reaction," he said. "Can you think of anything unusual you may have eaten in the past twenty-four hours? Have you taken any medicines? It's strange that you have no history of anything like this before."

"No," I told him miserably. "I'm not taking medicine and I haven't eaten anything I haven't eaten a hundred times before. How long will I be this way?"

"Not long, I hope," he said kindly. "This medicine is usually quite effective. Twenty-four hours should do it. If it doesn't, phone me and I'll change the dosage."

"Twenty-four hours!" I cried. "But there's a dance tonight! I've been counting on going for weeks!"

"That's a shame," Dr. Morgan said, "but it's not the end of the world, now, is it? At your age there's always another dance."

I could have kicked him. In fact, I really might have if my poor swollen feet hadn't been wedged so uncomfortably into the slippers.

When we got home Julia was finally up and dressed, and I broke the news to her as soon as I saw her.

"What I have is hives," I told her, "and they're

not going to get better before tomorrow, so the dance is off. I'm going to call Mike at work and leave a message for him at the pool office. I wouldn't let him see me like this for anything."

"I've seen people like that before," Julia said. She regarded me with interest. "The mountain people call it 'the crud.' What does it feel like? Does it hurt much?"

"No," I said, "but it itches like crazy." I turned to Mother. "Where do you keep the baking soda?"

"I'll get it for you." She frowned thoughtfully. "I hate to see Julia miss this dance, Rae, just because you aren't going to be able to go. Isn't there some way she can go without you? It's such a nice chance for her to meet some young people. Couldn't she go with Carolyn and her date?"

"I don't know," I said. "I suppose she could. I'll phone Carolyn and ask her."

"Please, don't," Julia said. "I've never met Carolyn's boyfriend, and I wouldn't feel right pushing in on them like that. Don't worry about it, Rachel. I really don't mind missing it. I'm not a very good dancer anyway."

And so it was settled, or I thought it was settled. I spent the day shut in the bedroom reading and trying not to scratch or in the bathtub soaking in baking soda. Every four hours I took a dose of medicine, and a few minutes later I would go and look in the mirror to see what result it was having. I suppose I had in the farthest back corner of my mind the tiniest ray of hope that the medicine would produce some miracle and that the transformation that had occurred in such a short time would un-occur just as quickly. It didn't.

At five-thirty I had just gotten out of the bathtub for what must have been the eighth time and was fastening my robe when there was a rap at the bedroom door and Pete's voice said, "Hey, Rae, can I talk to you a minute?"

"I guess so," I said without enthusiasm. The fewer people I saw at this point the happier I was.

I went over to the door and opened it a crack, and he shoved it the rest of the way open and came on in.

"Wow!" he said, doing a double take. "You really do look bad! I thought Bobby was exaggerating."

"Thanks a heap," I said, not inviting him to sit down. "What is it you want?"

"Well, look." He seated himself on the end of one of the beds anyway. "I wanted to ask you—say, can we shut the door?"

"Why?" I asked curiously.

"I just want to talk privately a minute, that's all."

I pushed the door closed and turned back to him. He was staring at the rug and drumming his fingers on his kneecaps, the way he did when he was feeling embarrassed.

"Look," he said finally. "Look, the whole thing I wanted to ask you was—well, couldn't Julia go to the dance tonight even if you can't?"

"Mother suggested that," I said, "and I told Julia I'd call Carolyn and see about Julia's going with her and Rick. She didn't want me to. She said she'd never even met Rick and it would make her feel funny."

"Do you suppose Mike would take her?" Peter asked hesitantly. "I mean, he's probably already got tickets and it's too late for him to have made any other plans. I could sit with them at intermission, and then afterwards I could bring Julia home."

"He would probably do it if I asked him," I said, "but I hate to put him on the line like that. Julia's our cousin, not his. It would be one thing if I were along too, but she's really not all that easy to talk to, and with nobody there to take up the slack he could feel pretty stuck."

"Nobody could feel stuck with Julia," Peter said firmly. "Girls don't have to jabber all the time to be good company. Besides, like I said, I'll sit with them at intermission and give Mike a chance to wander around and talk to people. And he won't have to drive her home or anything."

"Well—" I said slowly. I didn't like the idea, but I didn't want to be horrid about it either. Mike was always a good sport about things that pertained to the family. We had often taken Bobby with us to movies, and once when Dad was out of town on business, he had even suggested taking my mother.

"Please," Peter said quietly. It wasn't a word that Peter used very often.

The tone of his voice startled me, and I glanced at him sharply. He was still staring down at the rug, and his face was flushed.

"Look, Sis," he said awkwardly, "this thing really matters to me. I—I want Julia there tonight. I want her to hear me play. I mean, it's one thing I can do, you know—blow a horn. I want her to see me up there on the bandstand doing my thing, and people applauding and—well—you know."

I did know. Quite suddenly I knew a lot more about Peter than he had meant to tell me. With an effort I restrained myself from reaching over to tousle the awful orange hair, so like my own, which he must hate just as much as I did. I wanted to hug his skinny shoulders and say, "You don't have to be a superman. A girl can love you just because you're Peter."

Instead I said, "Okay."

"You mean, you'll ask Mike?"

"I said 'okay,' didn't I?"

"Gee, Rae, thanks." He let his breath out in a deep sigh and for the first time since the conversation started he looked up and met my eyes. "A first cousin isn't all that close, do you think, Rae? I mean, it's hardly any blood kin at all."

"In some states they're not allowed to marry," I told him.

"Marry! Who's talking about marriage? At least —well, if something like that came up it would be pretty far in the future, after college and everything. You don't worry about that sort of thing until you're right to it."

He got up and crammed his hands into his pockets and squared his shoulders. In his mind he was already at the dance, standing on the bandstand, raising the clarinet to his lips. Across the dance floor Julia was seated at a table, her gaze glued upon him, those huge dark eyes shining and wide.

"Pete?" I said as he reached the door. He turned back to me. "Do I really look as bad as—as—I think I do?"

Peter stood silent a moment, deciding whether to be kind or to be honest. Honesty won.

"Yep. I'm sorry, but it's pretty bad. Like you've dyed your face red and have lumps of chewing gum under your skin."

"Thanks," I said flatly, and wondered how I could ever have thought of hugging him.

I caught Mike at his home. He had gotten the message I had left for him at the pool office but hadn't taken it seriously. Now I told him I definitely wasn't going but that Julia would still like to.

He was regretful but cooperative.

"I don't mind taking you with lumps," he said, "but if you don't want to make the scene, that's okay too. As long as Pete will take over at the end of the evening, I don't mind doing the escort bit for your cousin."

"The doctor says I'll probably be okay by tomorrow," I told him. "We can plan to do something then." I tried not to sound as forlorn as I felt. Rachel, you good sport, I told myself, you're really one outstandingly unselfish girl!

Later, at the dinner table, that sportsmanship was really put to the test. Julia asked if she could borrow my new dress for the evening.

"I thought you were going to wear your yellow," I said. "The one you wore your first night here."

Julia wrinkled her nose. It was an expression she had picked up from Carolyn.

"That thing?" she said with a note of disgust in her voice.

"It's a pretty dress."

"Not on me, it isn't." She shook her head decidedly. "It's not my type and it doesn't fit right. The color's wrong too; it makes me look greenish."

I felt like saying, "Why did you buy it then?" I felt like slamming the water glass down on the table and shouting, "No! No, you certainly may not wear my new dress! I haven't even worn it yet myself!" I felt like doing a lot of things, all of them loud and rude and awful, but I sat and listened to Mother saying, "Why, I'm sure Rae won't mind lending it to you, dear, since she won't be wearing it. Do you think it will fit?"

"I think it will," Julia said. "Rachel, may I?"

They were all looking at me, waiting expectantly —Mother, Dad, Peter, even Bobby who was waiting for the question to be settled so he could ask for more potatoes. There was nothing I could say except what they wanted me to say.

"Yes," I told her.

When I saw her, however, actually wearing the dress, it was almost more than I could bear. It *did* fit Julia as though it had been made for her. The loose-fitting bodice was not loose on her but fit perfectly across the soft curve of her breasts. The shoulder seams fell at the right places and the short swirled skirt showed her long, shapely legs to marvelous advantage. And the color—the color was Julia; the pink reflected in her cheeks and made her eyes glow like two deep, dark, mysterious ponds.

Her lips curved slightly and she asked, "How do I look?"

"Beautiful," Mother said softly. "You look just beautiful. I can remember your mother at your age, dressed for a summer dance. She was beautiful too, but so very different—"

"Leslie," Dad interrupted gently, "do you really think this is the time?" and Mother said, "No. No, of course it isn't. Julia, darling, I'm sorry. How thoughtless of me! This is to be a happy evening for you and here I am, reminding you—"

"That's all right," Julia told her.

It *was* all right. I looked into her eyes, and it

was there, the look I had seen that first morning when I had wakened and glanced across and she had been lying on her back, gazing up at the ceiling. It was a quiet look, peaceful, pleased. A look of self-confidence that left no room for grief.

She doesn't care! Terrible—incredible—the knowledge swept upon me. Her parents are dead, and we're all so sorry for her—but to Julia, Julia herself, it doesn't matter! We think she's so brave, but she isn't brave—*she just doesn't care!*

Eight

When Mike arrived I did not stay to see him. Instead I went through to the kitchen and slipped out the back door into the yard. The moon hung huge and yellow about halfway up the curve of the sky, and by its light I could clearly see the tree to which Trickle was tied and his water bowl and the sad little heap that was Trickle himself. He had crept over to the edge of the hydrangea bush, but the rope wasn't quite long enough for him to get underneath it, and so he lay half in moonlight, half in the bush's shadow.

I said, "Trick?"

He lifted his tail politely and let it fall, but made no attempt to get up.

I went over to him and sank down beside him in the cool grass and stroked his back. His hair felt strange to my hand, lifeless and dry, and when I reached to scratch him behind his ears he raised his head and turned it to lick my hand. His nose felt warm and rough.

"You're sick," I whispered. "Poor little thing, I should have guessed it sooner. If you were feeling good you wouldn't have bitten anybody, even Julia. I'll take you to the vet tomorrow and get you dosed up with medicine. Then you'll be your old self again and you can come in the house and everything will be like it always was."

I sat with him a long time there in the moonlight, petting him and talking to him. When at last I went back into the house it was after ten. Mother and Dad were in the den, I could hear their voices, but I didn't stop to speak to them; I knew that if I heard either one of them comment on how pretty Julia had looked tonight and how brave and wonderful she was, I would not be able to stand it.

I went upstairs and put on my pajamas and got into bed to read. It was nice to have the room to myself again, as I had had it for so many years prior to Julia's arrival. As I reached over to get my book from the table between the beds, I was surprised to see that the base of the reading lamp, which was shaped like a cup, was filled with burnt matches.

"For gosh sakes," I said softly to myself. "Where could these have come from?"

I leaned over further and saw two empty match books stuck down on the far side of the lamp. They must be Julia's, I thought, but what could she have used them for? Could it be that Julia smoked? It seemed unlikely, for I had never detected the odor of cigarette smoke on Julia's person or in the room itself after she had been alone in it.

Still, why else would she be lighting matches?

I opened my book and tried to concentrate on the words on the page in front of me, but my mind

would not focus. The question of the matches both-
ered me too much to let it drop. If Julia did have
cigarettes she would have to keep them in the
bureau, for there was nowhere else that she could
store things. The bureau was, after all, mine as well
as hers. Just because Julia kept her things in two
of the drawers didn't exactly make them private
drawers, being as how they were part of a piece of
furniture that had been mine since childhood.

Hurriedly, before I could feel any guiltier about
it than I did already, I laid my book aside and got
out of bed and went over to the bureau and pulled
open the top drawer. All I could see at first glance
was a neat pile of underthings and a pair of pajamas. Gingerly I reached in and lifted the pile of
clothing to run my hand underneath it.

There were no cigarette packs.

I was beginning to feel disgusted with myself,
but having started the investigation I could not
stop. I ran my hand down the side of the drawer
to the back, and then I did feel something. It was
smooth and hard and had the same feel as a candle.

I pulled it out and looked at it. It wasn't exactly
a candle, for it had no wick, but it was a brown,
waxlike substance which had evidently been
melted and molded into an oblong shape with four
stubby appendages forming a kind of stand for it.
At one end there was another such protrusion,
shaped somewhat like the head of an animal.

"What in the world!" I exclaimed, regarding the
little wax figure with bewilderment. It was the sort
of thing one might expect from a child modeling
with clay, but the wax had melted and run together so that the shape was indistinct. As I turned

it over and over in my hands I saw something else strange. Several long, white hairs were embedded in the wax.

I was still examining it when through the open window I heard the sound of a car pulling into our driveway. Guiltily I thrust the wax figure back into the spot in which I had found it and shoved the drawer closed. I was in bed with my book in my hands when footsteps sounded on the stair. One pair of footsteps.

One?

I lay still, listening, as they came opposite the door and continued on down the hall. I recognized those footsteps, and they were not Julia's.

Shoving back the covers, I got up again and went to the bedroom door and opened it. At the far end of the hall, Peter was entering his own room.

I said, "Pete?"

He paused, but he did not turn around.

"Peter," I said, "where's Julia? I thought you were going to be the one to bring her home."

"Yeah. I thought so too." He did turn now and looked not at me but past me, as though by not meeting my eyes he could conceal the hurt in his own. "I guess my horn wasn't cool enough to make up for the rest of me. When the dance was over I went to find her, and she wasn't there. They took off during intermission."

"They?"

"Julia and Mike, who else? That's some great boyfriend you've got, I'll tell you. I thought he was going to introduce her around and see she met a bunch of people. They never spoke to anybody all evening, and when I went over to the table at the first band rest they were so wrapped up in each other they acted like they didn't even know I was there."

"No," I said. "I don't believe that. Mike just took her tonight because I asked him to do it as a favor. You're just telling me this because—because—"

But there was no ending for the sentence. There was no reason for Peter to tell me this if it was not true. Besides, the pain in his voice was equal to my own.

"I'm sorry, kid," he said and opened his door and went into his room, and I went back into mine.

Julia did not come in until close to dawn, and when she did I lay quiet with my back toward her, feigning sleep, because there was nothing I could say to her that would help in any way, and I knew if I tried to speak I would start to cry.

When I think back, I don't think I slept at all that night. I was aware of all the soft night noises —a tree rustling ouside the window, a lone car passing along the street in front of the house, Julia's heavy, even breathing in the bed across from me, for she fell asleep at once and never stirred again.

I did not sleep—and yet, I think I dreamed. Is that possible? No, of course not, and so I must have slept a little without realizing it, for in the dream I was running along the edge of a winding road. There were stark, red cliffs on one side of me and on the other there was a drop-off into a deep valley. My legs ached and my breath was coming in gasps, and I cried to Mike who was running beside me, "Will we get there in time? Can we get there before it happens?"

He said, "Are you crazy, Rae? If you'd only explain—"

"I can't!" I cried. "There's no time!"

Up ahead, far far ahead, a tiny reflection of the bright noon sunlight signalled the approach of a car coming directly toward us down the road.

"Stop!" I screamed. "Stop!" And in the dream I ran straight into the middle of the road with my arms outspread. The car came roaring toward me, and I was able to look directly into the eyes of the driver, wide, familiar eyes that recognized me as I did them.

Then, as with most dreams, before the ultimate climax occurred the dream was gone, and I was lying stiffly in bed, watching the sky outside the window lighten and turn pale and soften into pink and brighten into orange and burst at last to shining gold as the sun appeared above the ragged edges of the Sandia Mountains. Birds began to sing in the trees outside the window as though someone had suddenly pressed a button to bring them to life, and I thought, it's morning. The long night is over, and it's morning, and I haven't slept at all.

I lay there a while longer, until the sun had risen into the branches of the elm tree. Then I got up and dressed. The face that looked back at me from the mirror over the bureau was my normal face, no longer splotchy and bloated. The hives were gone as though they had never existed. I was Rachel again.

I went down the stairs and through the silent house and outside into the backyard. Trickle was still sleeping in the grass beside the hydrangea bush. I could see him there, a soft shadowy mound, curled just as I had left him the night before.

I crossed into the Gallaghers' yard and went up and rapped on the kitchen door.

Mrs. Gallagher opened it. She was a bright, cheerful woman, a little on the plump side, with Mike's blue eyes.

"Hello, Rae," she said with a smile. "You're up bright and early for a girl who was out most of the night. Does your mother need to borrow something for breakfast?"

"No," I said, trying to smile back at her. "She and Dad aren't even up yet. I just wanted to speak to Mike before he left for the pool."

"I'll call him." She held the door wide and called back over her shoulder, "Mike, Rachel's here!"

"I'll be down in a minute," Mike's voice called back from somewhere in the upper region of the house.

It was a good deal more than a minute. In fact, it seemed like hours as I sat at the kitchen table in the Gallaghers' pleasant kitchen, sipping at the glass of orange juice that Mike's mother had forced into my hand and trying to make polite conversation.

When at last he appeared in the doorway, Mike was wearing his swimming trunks and his T-shirt with "Coronado Club" across the front, and he had a towel draped around his neck.

"I've got to run," he said. "I have to hose down the sun area and set out the deck chairs before the pool opens."

"You might say 'good morning,'" I said.

"Good morning, Rae." He spoke the words in my direction, but his eyes flicked past me, unable to focus on my face.

"I'd like to talk with you," I said, "before you go."

"I don't have time," Mike began, and then—"Okay, but it'll have to be fast. Why don't you walk out to the car with me?"

So we walked out to the car, side by side with our arms swinging but not swinging together, our hands not touching, with the bright morning sunlight warm upon our shoulders and the back of our necks and the birds still singing away in a joyful chorus high over our heads.

Neither of us spoke until we reached the car, and then Mike said, "I guess you want to know what happened."

"Yes," I said. "I think you ought to tell me."

"I would if I could," Mike said. "I just don't know myself. I never had anything like this happen before."

"Are you in love with her?" I asked. I knew the answer, but I had to ask.

"It happened so fast," Mike said. "We didn't plan it or anything, Rae. It just happened like—well, like being hit by lightning."

"The way it was with us?"

"No, not that way at all. You and I—we just sort of grew into the thing. I mean, we'd known each other so long, and it was a friendship thing first, and then it got to be more. But with Julia and me it was like an explosion the first time I put my arm around her to dance. I'm sorry, Rae." He did look at me now and those honest blue eyes were wide and bewildered and guilty and happy and worried and sad, all at one time. "I never wanted to hurt you. I wouldn't have hurt you for anything if I could have helped it. You're—well, you're a great girl."

"Sure," I said. "Thanks a heap."

He stood there by the car with his hand on the door handle, looking down at me uncertainly. "Can we still be friends?"

"I've got plenty of friends already," I told him. "I don't need another casual friend."

"You don't have to be nasty."

"I'm not the one who's nasty," I said, my voice trembling. "I'm not the one who goes around snatching other people's boyfriends. It was my pink dress she was wearing—my new dress!" It was a stupid thing to say, but I could see her there in my mind's eyes as she must have been at the dance with her face lifted to Mike's and that thick black hair falling rich and soft over the pink fabric over which I had worked so long and hard. "I ran a sewing machine needle through my finger making that dress!"

"Now you're being silly," Mike said, sounding relieved because I suppose he had been afraid that I would cry. "The dress had nothing to do with anything. Hey, what happened to the hives you were supposed to have had last night? You look just like normal."

"They disappeared overnight," I said bitterly. "That's one thing hives and boyfriends seem to have in common."

It was a wonderful parting line, and I turned quickly and walked back across the lawn to my own yard, hoping it would ring in his ears all morning. I did not feel like crying. I was far too angry to cry. I wanted to scream and stamp my feet. I wanted to go upstairs and haul Julia out of bed and yank all that black hair out of her head. I wanted to untie my dog and take him up to the room where Julia lay, vulnerable and defenseless, and dump him on top of her and let him bite her. Or, if he didn't do that, he could at least growl and scare her. Anything he did would be better than nothing.

Well, why not, I asked myself. It's my room, isn't it, and Trick's my dog. I guess I can have my own dog in my own room if I want him there, and if Julia doesn't like it she can move out!

"Trick," I called. "Hey, Trickle! Here, boy!"

He was still lying there in a little hollow of grass at the edge of the bush. When he did not move I went over to him and knelt down beside him and touched his back. There was a strange rigidity about it.

I rolled him over on his side, and his head flopped limply, and I knew that he was dead.

Dead!

I had never known anything that had died before. Oh, I had seen dead birds lying on the lawn, tiny ones that had fallen out of nests and once a larger one who had flown into a plate glass window. Back when Bobby was little and had kept turtles, they had all died at once because of some strange turtle disease, and I had once seen a cat that had been run over in the street. But there had never been anything of my own that had died, never anything I had loved, and for a while I could only kneel there numbly stroking the soft white coat, unable to accept the fact of death.

"I'll take you to the vet tomorrow," I had told him. I would never take him anywhere now. Not to the vet. Not to the park for a run. Not to my room to lie patiently beside the desk as I studied. There would be no more use for the red plastic dishes that held his food and water or for the blue

collar with the name tag that read—TRICKLE. I BE-
LONG TO RACHEL BRYANT, 1112 DAKOTA NE.

He's gone, I thought incredulously.

I knelt there a long time, and finally I got up and
went into the house.

There was a pot of coffee on the stove which
meant that Mother was up and about, and an
empty cereal dish on the table which meant that
Bobby was also. From the den I could hear the
television blaring out the awful Saturday morning
cartoon shows that Bobby loved now as much as
he had when he was the right age for them. There
was no sign of my father, so I knew that Mother
had left him sleeping and was probably trying to
get some film developed before she had to come in
and fix breakfast.

I went out to the garage and rapped on the darkroom door.

"Don't come in," Mother called from inside. "I
have film exposed."

"Trickle's dead," I told her through the door.

"What?" There was a pause, and then Mother's
voice said, "Oh, honey!" There was the sound of a
locker opening and closing as the film was shut
away, and then the door opened and Mother
emerged with a look of shock on her face.

"Are you sure?" she asked.

"I'm sure."

"Oh, honey, how dreadful!"

She reached out to put her arms around me, but
I pulled back, not wanting to be touched.

"You made me tie him out in the yard," I said.
"You and Dad made me do that. He died of grief
because he thought nobody loved him any longer."

"I can't believe that," Mother said. "He must

have been very sick. That would explain why he bit Julia. That seemed so strange—so unlike him. He was always such a friendly little dog until then."

"He's out in back, still tied up," I said.

"Oh, dear." Her forehead crinkled into worry lines as she tried to decide what to do. "I suppose we should cover him with something."

"I'll do it," I said. "I don't want anybody handling him but me. I'm the only one who loved him. All the rest of you hated him because he bit your precious niece, your sneaking, two-faced, darling Julia!"

I felt the tears trying to come, and I fought against them.

"Rachel, dear," Mother said, "I know how upset you are, but you mustn't say such things. Julia has been through grief too, you know, a far worse grief than this. She's a brave, wonderful girl—"

"She's hateful!" I spat out the word. "She's a horrid, hateful witch! I bet she killed Trickle herself by—oh, doing *something*. Maybe she put poison in his water bowl!"

"Rachel!" Mother's face went white.

"She could have done it!" I cried. "She's bewitched all of you—Pete and Bobby and you and Dad and Carolyn—and Mike. Even Mike! That's why Trickle bit her! Dogs can judge people better than anyone—they know when somebody is horrid!"

The storm broke within me and the flood of tears came, pouring down my face, running salt into my mouth, and I turned and started back into the house, planning to run up to my room and throw myself across the bed and weep it all out until I could think clearly again. Then I remembered that the room was no longer my own. I could not possibly go into it with Julia there, and where else was there? I was locked out of my own house as truly as Trickle had been.

Whirling on my heel, I stumbled blindly in the other direction, out the garage door into the yard, and flung myself face down in the grass beside the body of my dog. I did not touch him now, for the shape that lay beside me was no more the real Trickle than a stuffed animal, and I buried my face in my arms and let the sobs come until I was too exhausted to cry any longer.

I don't know how much time passed before I heard Bobby's voice saying, "Rae?"

I lifted my head, and he was standing over me, his light brows drawn together in a solemn look that might have been funny in another time, under other circumstances.

"Rae," he said, "do you want me to bury him for you?"

"No," I said sharply. The finality of placing Trickle in the ground and covering him over with dirt was more than I thought I could bear.

"We've got to," Bobby said practically. "It's summer, and you know how it is in the summer. We could have a funeral—remember the way we did for my turtles?"

"I don't want a funeral," I said. "I'll bury him myself." And then, seeing Bobby's face, I realized that he was almost as upset as I was. Next to me, he had probably loved Trickle more than anybody in the family had.

"You can dig the hole," I told him.

So he got a spade and dug a grave in the corner

of the yard out by the rose bushes, and I went in and got a box which had once contained dark-room equipment. It wasn't a real funeral, but as he covered over the box Bobby said, "Don't you think we should say a prayer?"

"I guess so," I said, so we recited the Lord's Prayer very softly, and then I broke a rose off the bush nearest the grave and sprinkled the petals over the loose earth, and it was over.

When we went back to the house the whole family including Julia was in the living room. They seemed to be having some sort of conference, for I could hear Mother saying something about "—terribly upset, of course—" and Dad saying, "—has to learn to face these realities, no matter how distressing they are."

I passed the door without pausing and went up to my room. Even when she wasn't in it, the room held the feeling of Julia's presence. Her bed was neatly made, as compared to mine, still a shambles from my restless night and early rising.

On impulse I went to the closet and pulled open the door. My pink dress was there on a hanger on Julia's side of the closet. Angrily I snatched it up and transferred it to my side, but it looked bright and strange and unlike any of my other clothes. I knew that I would never wear it. The essence of Julia clung to every fold of the material; somehow in one wearing she had claimed it for her own.

"Witch!" I whispered. "Witch!"

Nine

My birthday is at the beginning of July.

I have always loved birthdays. I have a chain of birthday memories that run all the way back to the year I was three, although Dad insists that no one can remember that far. I got a doll for that birthday; she had real hair, not the painted kind, and was dressed in a ballet skirt, and when I took her out of the box I thought she was alive.

So, you see, I do remember.

Later there was a circus birthday when I saw my first elephant and ate my first cotton candy. And there was the bicycle birthday, and the tennis racket birthday, and when I was twelve there was the birthday that brought Trickle.

But this particular birthday, the one on which I turned sixteen, there was no air of festivity. This was my own fault, for my parents wanted to give me a party.

"Sixteen is such a special age," Mother kept saying. "Don't you want to invite some people to celebrate? Or if you'd prefer to have it just family, we could go out for dinner someplace nice and then maybe to a play."

"No," I told her. "I really don't feel like doing anything. I've outgrown that sort of thing."

The truth, of course, was that I would not share my birthday with Julia.

Julia. Just the sound of her name was enough to make me feel slightly sick. When I heard my Mother speak it, her voice filled with warmth— "Julia, dear, you really must do some posing for me. It's a waste to have a beautiful niece and not to use her for a model"—my stomach churned.

"Julie," my father called her. Every time he saw her his face brightened, as though she were the second daughter he had always longed for.

I held myself apart from them all and watched, and it was a strange feeling, as though I were a visitor from another planet observing something of which I was no part. I watched Julia smiling at my father and calling him "Tom." I watched her helping Mother in the kitchen, moving deftly about with a pan or a dish towel, taking over chores that formerly were mine. I watched Bobby tease her into a game of dominos and saw Peter's eyes follow her about with a kind of hopeless adoration.

But worst of all was watching her with Mike. For the first time in my life I wished that he did not live next door to us, for it made it much too easy for him to wander over after work, for no special reason, to sit on the porch steps and chat. He was as nice to me as he always was—nicer, really—for he no longer tossed me playful insults or called me silly nicknames. He was politely formal and very kind.

"You look really nice today," he would say. "I like your hair like that," although my hair was no different from what it had always been, "Is that a new outfit?" when I was wearing the same tired pair of denim shorts and faded plaid shirt that I had worn all summer the year before.

But he was not kind enough to try to hide his reason for coming.

"Is Julia around?" he would ask, avoiding my eyes. And Julia always was.

"You're not mad, are you, Rae?" she asked me. "It wasn't as though I could help it. These things do sometimes happen."

"You *made* it happen," I said bitterly. "You knew Mike was mine."

"He wasn't yours," Julia said in a reasonable way. People don't own other people. You told me yourself the first day I was here that you weren't going steady. I didn't break anything up. Mike says you were just good friends, that you've always been like a little sister to him."

"That's not true." I tried to speak with dignity. "He may say that now, but he wouldn't have said it a month ago."

"Things change," Julia said with a shrug.

This could not be denied. Things did change, and the thing that seemed to have changed the most was Julia herself. When I think back now, it is hard for me to decide exactly whom to picture when I say the name "Julia." There were three Julias—all different. There was the Julia who arrived with my parents that first day, hesitant and frightened, the haunted, tight-faced girl who stood uncertainly in the doorway in the shadow of my father, and held out her hand to me and said, "Hello." Then there was the later Julia, relaxed and self-confident, the quaint touch of the hills gone from her speech. This was the Julia who plucked her eyebrows so that they no longer hung like bushes over her huge eyes and used my lip gloss to widen her mouth and make her thin lips fuller and warmer. This Julia laughed and chattered and used Albuquerque slang and went with Carolyn to the hair dressers' and had her thick mane cut and styled into a long shag.

"She's copied Carolyn," I remarked to Peter, who immediately bristled as though he had been personally insulted.

"You're jealous," he said. "You've turned into a real cat since Mike threw you over."

"Threw me over!" True though they were, the words cut me to the core. I could not believe that my brother had said them. "What about you? Do you feel thrown over?"

"I never went with Julia."

"But you would have if you could," I said cruelly. "You fell for her like a ton of bricks, and you know it. And you're not over it either."

"So?" Peter said. "That's why I understand how Mike feels about her. No guy in his right mind could help falling for a girl like Julia, and she's got a right to choose anybody she wants. It burns me up to hear you run her down just because she has something that you haven't."

"What is it she has?" I asked, really wanting to know. "What are the qualities that have you and Mike so enchanted?"

"I can't explain it," Peter said. "It's just—something. A kind of feeling. A sort of—magic." And he blushed, embarrassed at having used a word that sounded so romantic. "She's just—special somehow."

This was the second Julia. There was a third Julia too. I would meet her later.

So, by my own request, there was no birthday celebration for me. I looked at myself in the mirror that morning as I was brushing my teeth and told myself, "You're sixteen now—sweet sixteen—the age when lovely things begin to happen." But nothing lifted and sang within me. At the breakfast table there were some packages waiting for me containing a blouse and some earrings and two record albums. I opened them and said my thank you's, but it was all rather flat and forced. I did not even feel like trying on the blouse, and instead of playing the albums I put them away.

In the middle of the morning Carolyn came by on her way out to the pool to ask if Julia and I would like to go with her.

"We can have lunch there," she said. "It's my treat because of your birthday."

"I don't feel like it," I said. "Thanks anyway."

Carolyn gave me a funny look and said, "Well, that's up to you. Are you coming, Julia?"

"Yes," Julia said, "as soon as I get my suit." She went upstairs and while she was gone Carolyn gave me my gift. It was a friendship ring with a tiny turquoise set in the silver band.

"I got it at Old Town a couple of months ago," she said. "I was so happy about finding it. I thought it was just the right present. Now—well, I don't know. Maybe you'd rather have something else."

"Of course not," I said. "It's lovely. Why would you think I wouldn't want it?"

"I don't know," Carolyn said again. "We just don't seem the same as we used to be. We used to talk about everything, but lately you seem to have sort of walled yourself off. You never want to go any place or do anything. I spend more time with Julia these days than I do with you."

"Then maybe you'd like to give the ring to Julia," I said shortly. As soon as I heard the words I wished I could call them back, they sounded so cold and bitter. I saw Carolyn flinch as though I had hit her. Carolyn and I had never in our lives said unpleasant things to each other. It was one of the proofs of our friendship that even when we argued we never got angry.

"I bought the ring for you," she said now in a tight voice. "You can keep it or exchange it or throw it away, it's all one with me. Here comes Julia now—you're dumb not to come to the pool. It's a beautiful day for swimming."

They left, and I went out into the yard and watered the roses. Then for lack of anything better to do, I strolled down the sidewalk and paused to say hello to Professor Jarvis who was sitting in a lawn chair in his front yard, writing in a note book.

"How did your talk go?" I asked him by way of greeting. "My father read in the paper that you were scheduled to give a lecture on witchcraft to some women's club."

"The University Women," he said, looking pleased that I had known about it. "It went very well indeed, thank you, my dear. It's one of the benefits of retirement to have the time to do such things."

"It's funny the University Women would be interested in such a fairy-tale subject," I said.

"A fairy-tale subject?" His pale blue eyes crinkled as he smiled. "Now there's where you're wrong, Rachel. The subject of my lecture had nothing what-so-ever to do with fairy tales. What I spoke about was modern day witchcraft of the sort that's practiced right here in this country all the time."

"You're kidding, of course!" I regarded him with amazement. "Nobody in this day believes in something like that!"

"No?" He laid his book down on his lap. "Then why is it, pray tell, that there are over four hundred witch covens in existence in the United States at this very moment?"

"You mean people who practice real magic?" I exclaimed.

"That depends upon your definition of 'magic,'" Professor Jarvis told me. "If you mean the fairy-tale stuff, then probably not. But if you accept as the definition of 'magic' the one originated by Aleister Crowley the question is debatable. Mr. Crowley is one of the best known of modern day witches, and he calls magic 'the science and art of causing changes to occur in conformity with will.' In other words, he describes magic as the utilization of the mind force to make things happen as they are desired."

"Do you think that's possible?" I asked doubtfully.

The professor nodded. "If I did not I would certainly not be giving lectures on the subject. We know that the mind has powers that often go undeveloped. Scientific tests conducted in laboratories have proved that certain people have more control over their mind forces than others. There are people who can predict the turn of a card or tune their minds in on events that are occurring at other places. Why then is it unreasonable to believe that there might be other people who can channel this mind force outward and *create* happenings instead of just know about them?"

"And such people are witches?"

"Some of them call themselves that."

"Have you ever really known one?" It was crazy, of course, but I was fascinated despite myself.

"I'm not sure, but I think so," Dr. Jarvis said seriously. "Back when I was first teaching at the University I had a student who came from a particularly secluded area of the Ozarks. Her name was Ruth, and she had been raised in an atmosphere of witchcraft, for her mother and aunts all claimed to be practicing witches. Whether this girl was one or not, she had been taught a number of charms which she used quite freely. She used to talk with me about it, knowing my interest in the subject.

"I remember one time in particular—" He smiled at the memory. "Ruth was in love with a young man who was a member of the basketball team. He was an extremely good looking boy and very popular. He dated one of the cheerleaders and as soon as they graduated they planned to be married. Well, Ruth decided to do something to offset that plan. She attended an after-game party in the cheerleader's dorm room, and while she was there she went into the bathroom and got a couple of hairs out of her rival's brush. She took these back to her room and made a little statue out of beeswax and stuck the hairs in it. Then she lit a match and began melting the wax figure. She let a couple of drops of wax fall, and then she blew out the match and went back to the party.

"Well, it just so happened that while Ruth was in her room performing this little ceremony, the cheerleader had become suddenly ill with stomach pains. The party broke up, and the basketball playing boyfriend was leaving just as Ruth reached the door. They stood in the hall and chatted a few minutes, and then Ruth suggested in a friendly way that they go back to her own room where she had a hot plate and could make some coffee. So they did, and she brewed the coffee and put something in it—I think she referred to the ingredient as 'milfoil,' but I believe it was actually a part of a plant called *Achillea millefolium.* From that night on, as far as I know, Ruth and the basketball player were a steady twosome, and he never looked at the poor little cheerleader again."

"What a story!" I exclaimed. "You don't really believe it, do you?"

"Well, I received it secondhand," Professor Jarvis said. "So I cannot be absolutely certain. What I do know is that Ruth herself believed it. As far as she was concerned it had a happy ending. She and her ballplayer married and moved to California where he played professionally for many years and finally retired to open his own sporting goods store. I still receive a Christmas card from them every year. They seem to be very happy."

"A wax doll," I said slowly. "She melted a wax doll."

"That's correct."

"Professor Jarvis—" I hesitated, hardly knowing how to ask the next question. "Was there anything about Ruth—about her looks—that made her different from other people? Was she especially beautiful?"

"No," the professor said. "In fact, she was quite ordinary looking. Very nondescript features, a short dumpy little figure. Nothing anyone would ever notice, except for her eyes."

"Her eyes?"

"She had strange eyes," Professor Jarvis said. "Sometimes they seemed opaque, closed over. Other times you would look into them and it would seem they were so deep they had no bottom. I think that if Ruth did indeed have powers of the kind she attributed to herself, her eyes were a focal point for them.

"And another odd thing—though she most certainly was not beautiful in any accepted sense of the word, there were those who swore that she was. The people who were closest to her, the ones on whom she concentrated her attention, seemed to see her with different eyes from the rest of us. They found her very beautiful indeed."

"Professor Jarvis," I said shakily, "do you know why I asked that question—about her looks—her eyes?"

There was a moment's silence.

Then the old man said, "I think I do."

"You met Julia," I said. "Could she—"

"My dear, I don't know. I did meet her, but only briefly. I must admit the eyes did startle me. They very much resembled Ruth's. However, there are many people in the world with vivid and interesting eyes. My own beloved wife had fantastic eyes, and the last thing she ever could have been was a witch. You simply cannot go around thrusting labels upon people because of physical characteristics which may mean absolutely nothing."

"But there are other things too," I said. "There is the wax figure! I found it one day in the back of her bureau drawer. I thought at the time that it was just an odd shaped ball, but there *was* a shape to it. It was elongated with a sort of knob at one end which might have been a head. There were four lumps sticking out at the corners like the legs of an animal—like the legs of a *dog*!"

"Rachel, my dear, you are jumping to conclusions," the professor said. "My story has disconcerted you. A lump of wax—"

"There were hairs in it!" I cried. "Hairs the color of Trickle's!"

"Rachel—" He raised a hand as though to hold back my words, but his eyes had taken on a certain sharpness that I had never seen in them before.

"Could you tell?" I asked excitedly. "If I brought it to you, could you tell?"

"Not definitely."

"But you would know if it was possible, wouldn't you? I mean, you've seen such figures before?"

"Yes, I have seen such figures. I would certainly have an opinion as to its authenticity, though an opinion is not proof."

"Then wait here," I told him. "I know right where it is—it will only take me a minute to get it!"

Without giving him a chance to reply I turned and began to run back along the sidewalk, past the Gallaghers' house and into my own yard. I bolted up the porch steps, through the front door, and up the stairs and down the hall to my room.

It was ridiculous. It was insane. But I could not

help myself. I had to find that figure and take it back to Professor Jarvis. Wildly I jerked open the top drawer of the bureau and began to rummage inside. I felt along both sides and under the piles of clothing. Then I removed the whole drawer and set it on Julia's bed and threw everything out of it.

The wax dog, if that was indeed what the figure had been, was gone, but I did find something else, so flat and thin against the base of the drawer that I would never have located it by touch alone. It was a photograph of me, one of the discards from the set of snow pictures that Mother had printed the month before. The face and body were covered with what appeared to be splotches of bright red paint.

Ten

I did not go back to Professor Jarvis that afternoon. Instead I phoned him and told him that I would be over to talk to him the following morning. I took the picture and glanced about for a hiding place for it and settled at last for sliding it under the mattress of my bed.

Then I went to the library.

To my surprise there was an entire shelf of books on the practice of witchcraft. I selected two of these with recent publication dates and carried them with me to one of the large round reading tables.

The first book was a sort of history, tracing witchcraft back to its early beginning as a form of worship of pagan gods and following it through the period of the Inquisition all the way to the present. During the time of the witch hunts over four thousand men, women and children were executed in Scotland alone, and in one year's time in Wurzburg, Germany, nine hundred supposed witches were burned alive. In our own country eighteen people were hanged in the town of Salem because they had been accused of being witches.

"At this point," the book reported,

> witchcraft appeared to vanish. In truth, it simply moved underground. In many backwoods and mountain areas it was still practiced and its secrets were handed down from one generation to another. The conjure words and doctrines could be passed only between blood relatives, and every woman who received this information did not automatically become a witch. Many were simply 'carriers,' keeping the knowledge alive until it eventually reached a person who had both the ambition and necessary psychic powers to put it to use.

It was the last part of this book that interested me most, for it dealt with the twentieth century, a time when laws against witchcraft were largely rescinded, and it began to emerge to public light in strange and unexpected places. I was startled to read that there was a coven of witches in Dover, England, during the Second World War who claimed to have used their spells and incantations to prevent Hitler from invading Britain. More recently two hundred fifty California mayors had met and been led in chants by a woman named Louise Huebner, the "official witch" of Los Angeles County, to cast a spell to help clean up the trash and litter on California beaches.

The second book was less factual. It was a collection of superstitions and beliefs concerning witches, collected by a man who had made the subject a kind of hobby. It told of such things as the woman who was said to have thrown a spell on a neighbor's tomato patch by drawing a circle in the dust, marking a cross in its center, and spitting upon it, and of another who disposed of her enemies by planting "hair balls" in their clothing. These balls were described as "bunches of hair mixed with beeswax and rolled into hard pellets." Another way in which a witch could cause death, according to this book, was to walk three times clockwise around a sick man. This was described as difficult to do because of the fact that most beds have at least one side against a wall.

An entire chapter of this second book was devoted to a witch's relationship with animals. The author seemed to think this extremely important.

"A witch can supposedly communicate with animals," he wrote, "and aligns herself with certain of these, particularly cats and wolves. The one animal which has a marked animosity to the witch is the dog. Superstition has it that a dog can recognize a practicing witch and will often react by attacking her. Because of this, witches seldom allow dogs on their premises and will go to almost any length to avoid them."

Could that be true, I asked myself? Could it really be true? My mind flew back to the day of Julia's arrival and the startled expression on her face when she first saw Trickle. "Please, keep him away from me!" she had cried, her voice going unnaturally shrill. "I mean it, Rachel!"

It could have been a coincidence. There were perfectly normal people who did not like dogs. But what of the reaction of Trickle himself, the sudden growl rising in his throat, and later the attack?

According to Carolyn there had been nothing to provoke it. Trickle had leapt upon Julia and bitten her as she had started up the porch steps. Had Trickle, with his animal instincts, sensed something that the rest of us could not? Was his attack upon Julia a valiant attempt to protect the people he loved by keeping her from entering our home?

There was no way to know except to face Julia with the question. In order to do this, however, I would have to present my suspicions in such a way that they could not be easily laughed away.

I spent the rest of the afternoon in the library reading both of the books from cover to cover. Then I checked them out and carried them home with me. I placed them on the table between our beds and waited for Julia to discover and comment on them, but she did not do so. After dinner, instead of going upstairs, she went to a drive-in with Mike.

Peter's band had an engagement that night, and I spent the evening in the den playing dominos with Bobby. Our parents were in the room with us, Dad reading in the recliner and Mother curled on the sofa, spotting prints and watching Lawrence Welk on television.

With Julia gone from the house everything seemed so miraculously easy and comfortable that I could almost believe that we were back again, relaxed and happy, in the era before she came. I looked across at my parents, noticing the little things about them that I usually took so for granted. The rugged, handsome features of my father's face could have belonged to a man years younger, but the hair above his ears was beginning to streak with gray. His hands were clean and strong, and the gold of his wedding band caught the light in odd little flashes as he turned the pages of his book. Mother sat in her own special position with her legs curled under her like a teenager. Her hair in the lamplight was the color of a pumpkin shell, and her tongue flicked out every now and then as she licked the spotting brush and inked out the dust spots on her pictures.

They were my parents, so much together and yet so individual, at times so infuriating, yet basically so wonderful. Now, watching their faces, I felt a surge of love for them so strong that it was almost physical in its intensity. It was the first really positive feeling I had had for a long time.

Mother must have felt it touch her, for she glanced across at me and smiled.

"Who's winning?" she asked.

"I am," Bobby said. "I only have two dominos left. Rae has five and she has to draw again."

"I don't have to draw," I told him. "I have a double six right here."

I placed the little wooden rectangle in its proper place in the domino formation, and Bobby bent his blond head, whistling through his teeth and studying his chances for cheating. I glanced again at Mother, who had turned her attention to her photographs. Does she feel it too, I wondered? Is she aware of the difference when Julia isn't here, the way the whole room seems to fill with love as though we're a real family again? The change in atmosphere was so dramatic that it seemed impossible that someone as perceptive as Mother would fail to recognize it.

"Mother," I said tentatively, "have you ever read anything about witchcraft?"

"Witchcraft?" She sounded surprised. "No, not recently. It seems to me my last experience with that subject was when Bobby was little and I used to read him to sleep at night with *The Wizard of Oz*."

"I mean real witchcraft," I said. "The kind that's being practiced in the United States right now."

"Honestly, honey," Mother said with a little laugh, "I have better things to do with my time than to read about silly things like that. I must admit though that I have enjoyed watching 'Bewitched' on television. Tom, did I ever tell you that I double-dated with Elizabeth Montgomery once when I was a teenager?"

"You've got to be kidding!" My father looked impressed. "How did that happen?"

"Well, my grandmother took me with her to a resort in New England one summer, and Liz Montgomery was there with her mother. We were the only young girls there, and we used to slip out in the evenings and party with the bellboys. She was so pretty—"

"As pretty as you?" my father asked teasingly. "Impossible!"

"Oh, Tom, you idiot!"

Mother giggled, and Dad said something else, and soon they were sparring back and forth, half kidding, half serious, their affection for each other flashing between them as brightly as Dad's wedding ring. This was something they had done ever since I could remember, and it had always made them seem to Peter and me so different from other people's parents. How long had it been since I had heard them do this, I wondered. Weeks? Months?

"Not since last spring," I said aloud. "Do you

realize that you haven't joked together since last spring?"

"Rae, really," Mother said lightly. "Who keeps track of things like that?"

"It hasn't been since Julia came," I said.

"Rachel!" The laughter left Mother's voice as quickly as it had come. "I simply will not listen to you say such a thing! It's not only ridiculous, it's downright malicious."

"But it's true," I insisted. "Think about it, Mother. You too, Dad; try to remember. Didn't things begin to change between us all when Julia arrived?"

"You seem to forget," Dad said, "that Julia's arrival was preceded by a tragedy that affected your mother and me deeply. Your mother lost her only sister whom she loved very much. If we haven't been in the mood for 'joking together,' as you put it, there has surely been a legitimate reason. Julia's arrival as a member of our family had nothing to do with it."

"Then why—" I began.

Mother interrupted. "This antagonistic attitude of yours toward Julia upsets us very much, Rae. Your father and I are at a loss as to how to handle it. I suppose it's natural for an only daughter to feel some resentment about sharing her place in the family with another girl, but you've never been a jealous sort of person. Knowing what poor Julia has been through, I should think you would feel enough sympathy to be willing to make a few sacrifices and do your best to make her happy in our home."

"Pete says that Rae's mad because Mike likes Julia better than her," Bobby contributed brightly.

"That's a lie!" I cried, and then, because it was not a lie and everyone knew it, I made matters worse by adding, "Mike Gallagher is nothing but a dumb slob!"

"If you have been using language like that, it's no wonder he prefers Julia," Dad said. "Any man, whatever his age, is turned off by vulgarity. I've never heard Julia raise her voice to anyone."

"You haven't?" I countered. "Well, then, you're lucky. You weren't around the day she screamed at Trickle. 'You vigrous, rat-fanged varmant!' she yelled, 'I'll warp you good!' You could have heard her all over the neighborhood!"

"That's absurd," Mother said. "Julia doesn't speak that way. Why, that's the kind of language you might expect from someone who has lived her whole life in the back hills. The little bit of Ozark color Julia's speech picked up from the summers she spent with her parents was lost almost immediately when she got here in Albuquerque."

"You can ask Carolyn," I cried. "She was there! She heard her! No, on second thought, don't ask Carolyn anything. She's on Julia's side just like you are. Julia's enchanted you all! She's got you wrapped around her little finger! I don't know what sort of spells she's cast, but with a witch like her—"

"That is enough!" I had seldom seen my father really angry. Now I found myself cringing before the absolute fury in his voice. "If there is anyone in this house who is behaving like a witch, it is Rachel Bryant! Go up to your room and stay there! We have all had just about all we can take of your viciousness toward your cousin!"

"I'll go," I told him. "I'll be glad to go! I just

wish it really was my room, all mine the way it used to be!"

I threw the last words back over my shoulder as I rushed from the den.

Once upstairs, I threw myself across my bed and wept into the pillow in a rage of anger and frustration. I could not really hate my parents. They believed the things they were saying. The Julia they knew was the one described in Aunt Marge's Christmas letter, "our angel Julie" who "filled the house with singing." How had Julia managed to conceal her true personality from her own mother? Or had she? Had Aunt Marge perhaps realized that her daughter was different from other people, that she practiced witchcraft and could work terrible enchantments? Or was one of these very enchantments the fact that she could keep those who were closest to her from seeing her as she was?

They were disturbing questions. As my storm of tears subsided, I tried to consider them in a calmer manner. How, I asked myself, had Julia been able to learn the practice of witchcraft in the first place? According to what I had read that afternoon, the doctrine could be passed only between blood relatives. Did this imply that Aunt Marge must also have been a witch and had received this information from my grandmother? If this were the case, it would mean that my own mother may have received it also. The picture of Mother melting wax figures and spitting into people's tomato patches was so incongruous that I could not consider it in any serious way. Besides, if she had been aware that the talent for witchcraft ran in our family, she would not have reacted as she had when I brought up the subject that evening.

I could find no answers that satisfied me. The pieces of the puzzle did not fit together, and yet I was becoming progressively more and more convinced that my suspicions were justified. The only way I would ever learn anything definite was to confront Julia herself.

I got up from the bed and went into the bathroom and washed the tear streaks from my cheeks. Looking at myself in the mirror, I recalled the way my face had appeared only weeks ago, splotched and bloated. Now it looked thin and pale and very determined.

"She's going to answer me," I told myself. "She's going to have to. I'll *make* her answer." How I was going to accomplish this I was not yet certain, but I did have one thing I could depend upon—the red spotted photograph that lay now, safely concealed beneath my mattress.

It was a quarter past eleven when I heard Mike's car pull to a stop in front of the house. It was almost midnight when Julia finally came inside. In the late night stillness I could hear the sound of the front door as it opened and closed and even the faint click as the latch was pushed into place. I heard Julia's footsteps on the stairs and then in the upstairs hall.

When she opened the bedroom door, I was standing, fully dressed, in the middle of the room, waiting.

"Why, Rae," she said in surprise. "What are you doing still up?"

"Waiting for you," I told her.

"For goodness sake, why? If your mother doesn't

feel it's necessary to check up on me, there's surely
no reason that you should."

"My mother is very trusting," I said.

Julia's eyes narrowed slightly. "What do you
mean by that remark?"

"I mean," I told her, "that Mother doesn't realize that you are a witch. I do, and I am able to
prove it."

The words came out as I had rehearsed them,
strong and certain. My voice was steady. I watched
Julia's face as I spoke and saw with satisfaction
the unmistakable look of shock. She covered it
quickly, but not quickly enough.

There was a moment of silence. Then Julia said,
"I don't know what you're talking about."

"Yes, you do," I said. "I'm talking about witchcraft, the kind that is practiced by a few very special people. With this sort of witchcraft a person
can cast spells with herbs and potions. She can
maim and kill by making wax figures to represent
her enemies, and she can cause a case of hives by
spattering red paint on another person's photograph."

"You must be crazy," Julia said. "You've never
seen me do any of those things."

"No, I haven't seen you actually do them, but
I've seen things that prove to me that you have
done them." I marshaled my facts. "I saw the wax
figure you made of Trickle and the matches you
used to melt it. I found the picture of me that you
used to bring on the hives. Those library books
over there on the table have filled me in on a lot
of things. I know, for example, why Trickle at-
tacked you and why you felt you had to kill him,
poor little thing. He recognized you for what you

were and tried to protect us. I know how you must have won Peter and Mike. You added something called 'milfoil' to whatever it was they were drinking when they were with you."

"Goodness, you've been studying hard," Julia said lightly, but the amusement in her voice was not reflected in her eyes. They seemed to grow deeper and darker with each passing second. "What do you think you're going to do with all this new-found knowledge?"

"I'm going to see that you leave Albuquerque," I told her. "I don't care where you go, whether it's back to school or to the hills where you probably learned all this stuff in the first place. What matters is that you get out of our lives and leave my family alone!"

"How do you think you are going to accomplish this?" Julia asked calmly. "Your parents are never going to believe you. As you say, your mother is 'very trusting,' and Tom is too. They love me and they're not going to listen to you making silly accusations."

"They'll have to believe me," I said. "I'll show them the picture. I may not have the wax figure of Trickle, but I do have the photograph."

"So?" Julia said. "What will that prove? Only that you are so determined to turn them against me that you spattered a picture with paint in order to pretend I did it. Your parents are so naive they wouldn't recognize witchcraft if they had it waved in their faces. Mike and Peter both will swear up and down that no kind of spell was worked on them. And as for that nasty little dog of yours, who is to say why he died? Maybe he choked on his own bad temper."

"My parents *will* believe me!" I cried angrily. "I'm not going to them alone with all of this. I'm taking somebody with me. He's a well-known authority on witchcraft and is respected by everybody. I've already talked to him about you. He'll stand behind me. He'll know what that picture means the minute he sees it."

"You don't know anybody like that," Julia said. "How could you? A dumb little girl like you doesn't have friends of that sort."

"Oh, don't I?" I was shaking with fury. "A lot you know! Professor Jarvis used to be the head of the sociology department at the University! My parents like and respect him, and they'll believe what he tells them!"

"I wouldn't be too sure of that," Julia said quietly. She smiled.

This time it was a real smile and showed in her eyes as well as on her lips. Something had happened during the final few moments of our conversation. Suddenly Julia was not worried at all.

Eleven

There was no way that night that I could have slept in the room with Julia. I took my pillow and crept downstairs to the den where I spent the rest of the night lying rigid and sleepless on the sofa.

It was close to dawn when I dozed off at last, and what seemed moments later I opened my eyes to find my father standing over me.

"I was leaving for work," he said, "and glanced in as I passed the door. Did you sleep here all night?"

"Most of it," I said groggily.

"Did you and Julia have an argument about something when she came in last night?"

"Yes."

"Will you tell me what it was about?"

"I'd rather not do that yet," I said. "It would just make you angry. You wouldn't believe me now. I want to talk with somebody else first."

"Daughter—" He made a little helpless gesture with his hands. "I can't figure you out. The way

you acted last night with your mother and me—
and then to fight with Julia—and to come down
here to sleep when you have a perfectly good
bed upstairs—it isn't normal behavior. Why can't
you tell me about your argument? You've always
felt you could discuss things with me before."

"All right," I said with a sigh. "I'll tell you. I
accused Julia of being a practicing witch."

"If you're making a joke," Dad said, "it's a taste-
less one. If you're telling the truth you deserve to
be punished. Did you really say something so
spiteful to your cousin?"

"See?" I said miserably. "You forced me to tell
you. I knew it would make you mad."

"Then you did say it?"

"Yes!" I hoisted myself to a sitting position on
the sofa. "I said it because it's true. She *is* a witch.
She all but admitted it to me straight out. She can
cast spells. She killed Trickle with one, and that's
how she won Mike."

"That is enough, Rachel. I won't listen to one
more word." Dad's voice was like ice. "Mother and
I have tried to be patient, but you have pushed us
past our limit. You and Julia may have such different natures that you don't get along well. I could
understand that and even sympathize with it. But
for you to go to these lengths to manufacture absurd accusations which you yourself admit are unbelievable is too much. Besides that, it's just plain
dumb."

"You're the one who's dumb!" I cried, pushed
past endurance. "You and Mother both refuse to
see what's right in front of your faces! This morning I'm going to talk with Professor Jarvis. He

knows about these things and will be able to explain them to you."

"You're not going anywhere except to your room," Dad told me. "You can spend your morning there thinking things over. If by noon you are not ready to apologize to Julia for your rudeness you can move out of the room entirely. I'm not going to have that poor girl subjected to any more scenes like the one you must have thrown last night."

"Where do you want me to move?" I asked. "Shall I sleep in the hall?"

"Cut the sarcasm, Rachel. There's an extra bed in Bobby's room. You could move in there. It would be an unfair thing to do to Bob, to make him share his small room with an older sister, but I don't see any alternative. That is—if you decide to move."

"I've already decided," I said. "But first I do have to see Professor Jarvis. It's terribly important, Dad, really. Couldn't I just run down to his house for a few minutes and then come back and be grounded?"

"Certainly not," Dad said shortly. "You've made your choice. Now get upstairs and don't let me hear of your stepping out of that room before noon. At that time you are to move your clothes to Bobby's closet."

I had no reply. Dizzy with anger and helplessness, I gathered up my pillow and climbed the stairs and went into my bedroom. Julia, dressed in jeans and the Indian shirt I had helped select, was standing in front of the bureau, brushing her hair. She did not speak, but her eyes met mine in the mirror, and she smiled.

"I'm changing rooms," I told her. "I'm taking all my stuff out of the closet including that pink dress I made."

"Oh?" The hand with the brush continued to move with sweeping strokes down the length of the shaggy black hair. "You might as well leave that. It doesn't fit you and the color's wrong. You made it for me, you know."

"I did not," I retorted. "You talked me into letting you wear it the night of the dance. I made it for myself."

"Oh?"

One lone word, spoken softly, almost smugly. I felt a cold shudder go through me at the implication of the question. Had I, in truth, made the dress for myself? I had thought that I had. And yet, I had purchased a pattern that was ill-fitting and unbecoming. I had chosen a color that I had never wanted to wear, yet one which looked beautiful on Julia.

My mind flew back to that day at House of Fabrics when we had stood, Julia and Carolyn and I, before a counter piled high with bolts of varied colors of material. There had been blues and greens and lavenders, shades which I knew were flattering to my coloring. I had looked past them as though they were not there and had reached instead for the pink.

"Julia, what are you choosing?" I had asked gaily, and Julia had said, "I don't sew. Besides, I don't need a new dress."

Of course, she had not needed a dress! I could see that now! *I* was to provide one. In total ignorance, I had sat on the den floor hour after tedious hour meticulously cutting and basting. Later I had sat at Mother's sewing machine and carefully stitched it together, the exact dress that Julia desired!

And I had not realized it! That was the most terrifying fact of all! I had thought that I was doing what I myself wanted to do. Now, suddenly, I was able to understand how it was that Mike was so convinced that the love for Julia that had befallen him was wonderful and natural. "It happened so fast," he had told me. "It happened like —well, like being hit by lightning!"

Now, turning to look at Julia, I said, "You won't get away with this." I struggled to keep my voice steady. "Not any of it. I can convince my parents, and I will."

"You do that," Julia said, "if you can." She laid the brush down on the bureau top and surveyed her reflection in the mirror. "I like my hair cut this way, don't you? It makes my face look—softer somehow. Mike likes it this way. So does your father."

"I don't like anything about you," I said coldly. "That includes your hair."

"How rude," Julia said. "You'd better not let your parents hear you say something like that. They'll be very upset with you, even more so than they are already." She flashed me another bright smile. "Enjoy your moving and be sure to leave me enough hangers. I'm going to get some breakfast."

She left the room, pulling the door shut behind her.

I sank down onto the edge of the bed, more disturbed than I had been the night before. I had imagined that with time to think the situation over Julia would have begun to realize the power of my position. I had a strong ally in Professor Jarvis, or at least I would have as soon as I was able to talk with him and fill him in on all the things that had happened. He would recognize the significance of the spattered photograph; he would know too about the spells that could be concocted from the contents of the jar that Julia had brought with her in her suitcase.

But that jar—I had not seen that since she had unpacked. And the picture—

I jumped up from the bed and lifted the edge of the mattress. The photograph that I had placed there was gone.

Gone, as though it had never existed, was the only real evidence I had. I was sickened by my own stupidity. Knowing what I did about Julia, how could I have left the picture in the room? For someone with her powers, locating a hidden photograph must have been child's play.

I released the mattress and let it fall back into place. The library books still lay as I had left them on the table between the beds. It was clear that Julia considered them unthreatening, or she would have managed to dispose of them also.

I went over and picked up the top book, the one about superstitions. What would Mother say if I carried this downstairs to her right now? Would she read it if I asked her to? I very much doubted it. My only hope was to talk to Professor Jarvis. Perhaps if I could get him to describe to my parents some of the things he had told me it would open their eyes to the possibility that I might be telling the truth.

It was then that I noticed a slight, acrid scent

in the air. A sulphur odor, as though someone had been burning matches.

Matches! I turned to the bedside table and there it was, a pile of burnt matchsticks stuck into the base of the lamp exactly as it had been before. I had wondered then what it was that Julia had been doing. Now I did not have to wonder. I *knew*.

For a moment I stood, stricken, too horrified to move. My heart was beating so hard that I could feel its pounding in my head. The matches—the lamp—the table, swam before my eyes.

So this was why Julia had seem so lighthearted in the face of my threats! She had no intention of letting me bring Professor Jarvis or anyone else to talk to my parents. Somewhere in this house at this very moment there was a little wax figure in which were embedded some orange hairs, taken no doubt from the brush on the bureau. Whenever she chose, Julia would begin to melt it.

Or had she begun to do so already? Even as I asked myself the question, a blinding pain shot through my head directly behind my eyes. Terrified, I staggered backward and fell upon the bed, clapping my hand against my temples.

She's doing it, I thought frantically. She has shut herself away in a closet somewhere and has lit a match, and at this exact instant she is holding it to the wax doll's head!

Yet that was impossible, for at that moment I could hear Julia's voice floating up from the yard beneath my open window. Struggling against my pain, I hauled myself up from the bed and crossed the room to look out. Yes, it was Julia, and she was talking with Bobby who had taken the mower out of the garage and was kneeling beside it, adjusting the blades.

I stood there, staring down at the two heads directly beneath me, the black one with the shag cut, the butter-colored one that was my brother's.

"—when you cross a parrot with a tiger?" Bobby was asking. "I don't know, but when it speaks, you'd better pay attention!"

He burst into uproarious laughter, the way he always did when he told idiotic jokes, and Julia's low, throaty laughter joined his.

"That's a good one," she said. "I never heard that one before."

The yard was filled with sunshine, and the roses along the back fence were a riot of pink and crimson. In the yard on the far side of the fence, I could see Mrs. Gallagher in her vegetable garden picking beans. It was all so peaceful, so innocent a setting. No normal person could look at a scene like that and think about destruction and evil.

What was it my father had said when he had come into the den to find me sleeping on the sofa? "It isn't normal behavior," he had told me, and there had been worry in his voice.

So I'm abnormal, I thought. Who wouldn't be under the circumstances?

The pain in my head had vanished. Evidently I had produced it myself with my own fear. That did not mean that next time it would not be real. At this moment Julia was standing in the yard, chatting with Bobby, but it would not be long before she went back inside. I could not watch her constantly. That would be impossible. Somewhere there existed a wax doll that bore my features, and I was not safe for a moment until I found it.

Would she have left it in the room? It seemed unlikely, but not impossible. It was with no hesitation this time that I pulled forth the bureau drawers and emptied out their contents, that I plowed through the closet and book shelves and tore the sheets from the beds. Without a trace of guilt I investigated the inside of Julia's pillow slip and rummaged through the pockets of her clothing.

By the time I had completed my search the room looked as though it had been hit by a cyclone, and I had discovered absolutely nothing.

I went again to the window. Bobby and the mower were gone now, but Julia was still there, standing in the same spot that she had been when I had last looked out at her. Her head was tipped sideways as though she was listening. She seemed to be waiting.

For what, I could not imagine, but I found myself waiting too.

In a moment it came. Bobby's voice shouted something from someplace down the street. I could not understand the words, but in the next yard Mrs. Gallagher could, for she dropped the basket with the beans and took off in a run around the side of the house. I had never seen plump Mrs. Gallagher run before. Under normal circumstances it might have been funny. Now the sight of it sent a stab of fear through me.

I left the window and hurried across the room and out into the hall.

"Mother!" I cried. "Something's happened!"

When there was no answer from the house below, I raced down the stairs and through the front door and out onto the porch. Mother was already in the yard, and Bobby was there with her, gesturing wildly, his eyes huge against the dead white of his face.

"Slow down, dear," Mother was saying. "I can't understand you when you talk so fast. What happened? You're not hurt, are you?"

"It's not me!" Bobby drew a long sobbing breath and forced his voice into a lower key. "It's Professor Jarvis! I went down to his place to mow his lawn. I rang the bell to tell him I was there, and he didn't come. He didn't answer the bell."

"Is that all?" Mother asked with relief. "For heaven's sake, Bob, there are all kinds of reasons why people don't answer doorbells. He might have been busy with his writing or taking a nap, or he might have had the television on—"

"I know," Bobby said. "I thought that too, so I tried the door. It wasn't locked. It swung right open. The professor was there, right there on the floor in the hall! His eyes and his mouth were open and he wasn't moving!"

I knew what his next words would be before he spoke them. If I could have I would have lifted my hands and covered my ears. But I could not move. I could simply stand there and listen.

"Mother—" Bobby said brokenly—"Mom—I think he's dead!"

Twelve_____

The next twenty minutes seemed to last forever.

By the time the ambulance arrived, half the neighborhood had congregated in the yard in front of Professor Jarvis's house. The only ones inside the house were Mrs. Gallagher and Mother, but people kept shoving up onto the porch, trying to see in the window.

"He hanged himself!" somebody shouted. "I can see the rope!"

Bobby, who was standing next to me at the edge of the sidewalk, shuddered convulsively. "There wasn't any rope," he whispered hoarsely. "He was just lying there in the hallway. Why are they saying there's a rope?"

"People just like to make things worse than they are," I told him, putting an arm around his shoulders. To myself I thought, there was no way anyone could make things worse than they were. The truth was more horrible than any conjecture.

When the ambulance came the crowd parted to

make a path for the men with the stretcher. Mother opened the door for them, and they went into the house. When they emerged a few moments later there was a blanket-covered form on the stretcher, and as they came opposite I could see a familiar shock of snowy hair protruding from beneath one end of the blanket. The attendants loaded the professor into the back and Mrs. Gallagher got in with him, and the door closed and they drove away. The thin wail of the siren lingered in the air long after the ambulance itself was gone.

With the excitement over, the crowd began to disperse, chattering eagerly, as though the thing they had just witnessed had been planned for their entertainment only. "—blood all over the place," the round-faced woman from across the street was saying. "He was literally lying in a pool of it! A regular Jack-the-Ripper case right here in our quiet neighborhood!" And another woman from further down the block was as firmly informing everyone who would listen that "he starved himself to death. Old people should not be allowed to live alone. They don't know how to take care of themselves properly."

I crossed the emptying lawn in front of the Jarvis home and went up the steps and in through the front door. Mother was standing at the hall phone, thumbing through a small leather-bound address book. She glanced up and asked, "Do you remember the married name of the Jarvises' daughter."

"No," I said, "but when he speaks of her he calls her Bonnie. I think she lives in Clovis." Shock had made my voice flat and strange. "Is he really dead?"

"No," Mother said. "There was a pulse beat but it was a faint one. The ambulance attendant said he thought it was a stroke." She flipped the pages of the book. "Here, this must be it—Bonnie Chavez in Clovis. Go see about Bobby, will you, Rae? I'll be home as soon as I make this call."

"All right," I said.

When I went back outside Bobby was no longer where I had left him, so I walked slowly along the sidewalk toward our own house with the vague, unfocussed feeling that I was moving through a dream. It's not real, I thought. I just talked with him yesterday!

The sidewalk was hot under my bare feet and above my head the leaves of the maples stirred softly in a breath of breeze. Professor Jarvis's petunias were blooming joyously along the edge of his driveway. Beyond the trees the summer sky arched blue and high, and some skinny little strips of clouds were drifting lazily in the direction of the mountains.

It can't be true, I told myself. If I once admitted that it was I would have to face the other fact as well—that I was the one responsible.

"I'm taking somebody with me," I had announced to Julia the night before. "He's a well-known authority on witchcraft." And I had not stopped there. I had gone so far as to call him by name.

"Professor Jarvis used to be head of the sociology department at the University," I had cried triumphantly.

Julia had smiled and it was no wonder. I had told her exactly what she needed to know.

I had been correct in my guess about the construction of the doll. My mistake had been in thinking that I was the intended victim. It was useful to Julia to have another girl around, someone whose friends she could captivate, whose clothes she could wear, whose ways she could copy. And it was easier by far to remove the professor who was the one person who could and would support my accusations. Without the help of Professor Jarvis I was helpless to convince my parents of anything.

And so because of my stupidity a wonderful man lay dying or perhaps by this time was already dead.

I turned into our yard and she was there on the porch, waiting.

My cousin Julia.

Bobby was with her, and I could tell by the puffiness of his eyes and the smudges on his cheeks that he had been crying. Julia had her arm around him as I had had mine only a short time before, and she was talking in a gentle voice.

"Things like this are bound to happen when people get old," she was saying as I came up the porch steps. "It's all for the best, dear. Nobody can live forever. He was a poor, sick, old man."

"He was not!" I exclaimed vehemently. "He was a healthy, vital, energetic person! He hasn't had a sick day in all the time that I've known him! He should have lived at least another fifteen years!"

"Oh, really?" Julia's eyes met mine across the top of Bobby's blond head. "Well, in that case, perhaps he will. You never can tell about things like that. Some people go on as vegetables for incredibly long stretches of time."

"As vegetables!" I gasped.

"Oh, you know what I mean. Not able to move or talk." She turned to Bobby. "Let's go inside, shall we? It's getting so hot out here. Why don't I fix us some lunch, and then we can play a game of dominos."

"I'm not hungry," Bobby said.

"Then we'll have the game first and lunchtime after." She got to her feet, drawing him with her, and I was amazed to see him lean his head back against her shoulder in a way he never did with anyone but Mother. He blinked his eyes hard and wiped his nose with the back of his hand and said, "Okay, I'll play you. But I don't really feel like it much."

"That's a good boy," Julia said warmly, and she even sounded like Mother. "You go wash your face and I'll find the dominos and get things set up."

They went into the house together, and I seated myself on the porch steps to wait for Mother. There seemed to be nothing I could do that would not make things worse. Nothing I said would carry any weight without the remains of the wax doll of the professor. Even if by some miracle I were able to locate it, there would be no one to support my conjecture that it was connected with what had happened.

My reverie was interrupted by the mailman who came swinging up the walk, whistling.

"Hi, there," he said jauntily. "I hear there's been some excitement on your block. They've been talking about it at every house I've been to."

"I guess you could call it excitement," I said. "I think a better word for it might be 'tragedy.'"

"It's a shame," the postman agreed, dropping his lighthearted approach. "The professor's a nice, friendly guy. Here's your mail, a good pile of it today."

"Thanks," I said as he dumped the letters into my lap.

As I glanced down at the pile I saw that the top letter was for my father and bore the return address of a law firm called Becht and Bristol. This surprised me because it was seldom that my parents received letters from attorneys. The only occasion I could remember was once when a magazine had used one of Mother's photographs without paying for it and there had been correspondence between Mother and the lawyer who represented the magazine. This could not be about something like that, for the law firm was a local one and the letter was addressed not to Mother but to my father.

Setting the mail on the step beside me, I leaned my head against the porch railing and refocussed my thoughts. If only it were possible to go back to yesterday and start over! But what was done could not be altered. At this point I could only pray that Professor Jarvis would recover. If Julia could channel her mind force to produce illness, I vowed that I would push mine as hard as I could to combat it. Perhaps a volley of positive thoughts all surging toward him at once would help the professor to hold out against the pressure Julia must be asserting from the other side.

I closed my eyes and concentrated.

"Get well!" I cried silently over and over in my mind. "Please, Professor Jarvis, get well! You must get well! You just *have to*!"

By the time Mother came up the walk I was still at it and completely exhausted.

"I got hold of the professor's daughter," she said, "and she and her husband are coming. It's a four and a half hour drive so they should be here the latter part of the afternoon. She was terribly upset and there was so little I could tell her."

I opened my eyes and let my mind relax."

"Should we call the hospital and see how he is?" I asked.

"Mrs. Gallagher's with him. The Gallaghers have been his next door neighbors for so long that she feels almost like a relative. She'll call us as soon as there is anything to report." She glanced at the pile of letters. "Is that today's mail?"

"Yes," I said, handing it to her. "Dad has a letter from a law firm."

"It's probably about the estate," Mother said. "Ryan named Dad the executor of his will and Marge's."

"What does that mean?" I asked. "Everything goes to Julia, doesn't it?"

"Yes, but there's a lot of red tape connected with settling an estate, even if there's only one person to inherit. It takes time to get things ironed out."

"Will Julia be rich?" I asked.

"Well, people's ideas of what constitutes 'rich' differ. She will be well enough off so that she can do pretty much as she pleases in regard to college and travel and things like that." She thumbed through the mail. "Here's something for Peter from

U.N.M. It must be about pre-registration. A check from *Discovery Magazine*—that will be for those Halloween pictures. Why, here's a letter for Julia!"

"For Julia?" I snapped to attention. "From whom?"

"Somebody named Mary Carncross in Boston. It must be a friend from her school. The letter was mailed to Pine Crest and forwarded here."

"She's never talked about any friend by that name," I said.

"I've never heard her talk about her school friends at all. Still, she must have them. She attended that boarding school for several years. It's nice to know that one of them—"

She broke off in mid-sentence at the sound of the telephone ringing inside the house.

"Do you think that's Mrs. Gallagher?" I asked, getting quickly to my feet.

"I hope so—with good news." Mother was only one step behind me as we hurried into the house.

It was indeed Mrs. Gallagher, but the news was short and inconclusive. In the opinion of the doctor who had examined Professor Jarvis, he had suffered a stroke. How serious it was could not be determined because he was still unconscious. Mrs. Gallagher was prepared to remain at the hospital until Bonnie Chavez arrived from Clovis and wondered if one of us would go next door and leave a note on the refrigerator for Mike and Mr. Gallagher.

"I'll take it over," I offered.

"All right," Mother said and then frowned. "Wait—didn't Dad say you were supposed to be grounded?"

"Only till noon," I said. "Besides, he didn't know

there was going to be an emergency. I've already been down to the professor's house, so this won't make it much worse."

"You're right, I guess," Mother said. "Go ahead. Put the time on the note so they know when it was written."

I went across to the Gallaghers' yard and around to the back and in through the kitchen door. I knew their house almost as well as I did my own. Mrs. Gallagher kept a pencil and pad of paper next to the telephone. I tore off a sheet and wrote out the message and attached it to the refrigerator door with one of the little magnets she kept there for this purpose.

Once inside the house I could not seem to get myself out again. I had not been over since the morning after Mike had taken Julia to the dance. Now, standing in the quiet of the sunny kitchen, I was besieged with memories that went back to a time long before Mike and I had started dating.

The cookie jar in the corner was the one Mike and I had raided when we were so little that we had had to drag a chair over to stand on to reach it. The pot holders on a hook by the stove were ones I had woven myself. The plant on the windowsill was the result of a Mother's Day shopping trip we had made together; in our own kitchen at home there bloomed another plant just like it.

Past the kitchen lay the dining room where I had sat as a guest on many occasions. Beyond that was the living room where Mike and I had spent evenings doing homework.

Knowing I had no right to, I walked slowly through the rooms that had been so much a part of

my childhood. In the den was the footstool Mike
had made in woodworking class in junior high
school. In the hallway at the foot of the stairs was
the spot on which I had been standing almost a
year ago the night when he first kissed me.

"You've got a smudge on your nose," he had said,
and reached out with his forefinger as though to
rub it off. And then, as I had stood there looking up
at him, the teasing look had gone out of his eyes.
His hand had moved from my nose to rest against
my cheek.

"You've grown up an awful lot all of a sudden,"
he had said softly. And then he had kissed me.

Afterward neither of us had known what to say.
We had stood staring at each other, only half hearing the sound of the television in the next room
mingled with the voices of his parents.

Finally he had said, "Was that—okay?"

"Yes," I had answered. "Very okay." And suddenly we were laughing and his arm was around
my shoulders, and it was like a beginning but also
like a continuation of something that had really
begun a long time ago.

"Mike says you were just good friends," Julia
had told me. "That you've always been like a little
sister to him."

That was not true. Standing in the hallway, remembering the look in Mike's eyes after that first
kiss, I knew it was not true.

I paused, and then, knowing there was no ex-
cuse for the thing I was doing, I went up the stairs
and down the hall to Mike's room. I stood in the
open doorway and looked in at it. His bed was
made, but only just barely, with the spread yanked
up over the lumps in the blanket. His swimming

trophies stood in a row on the bookcase—I had
been there when he had won most of them—and
a batch of sports magazines were piled on the floor
by the side of his bed along with a ragged pair of
tennis shoes with socks still in them and some
empty coke cans and an open bag of potato
chips.

I turned my gaze to the bureau. There, to my
surprise, was my class picture, the one I had given
him in exchange for his, plus a couple of snapshots taken the summer before on a picnic at the
lake. In one I was standing on the bank in my last
year's swimming suit, skinny and freckled and
laughing, my eyes squinted against the glare of the
afternoon sun. In another Mike and I were together, wearing silly sailor caps and making faces
at the camera.

So he had kept the pictures. It was something I
had not expected, but when I thought about it
there was no real reason why he would have
thrown them away. They were part of a time that
he might someday enjoy remembering. He had
probably not yet gotten around to transferring
them to a scrapbook or to the back of a drawer.

I turned away from the room, both glad and
sorry that I had looked into it. The pain of loss was
more acute than ever, but there was something reassuring in the fact that Mike himself was the same
as he had always been, that he still munched potato chips while he was reading and dumped magazines on the floor and left his socks in his tennis
shoes.

Perhaps someday, I thought, I'll be able to feel
sisterly toward him. I'll be fond of him in the same

way I am of Peter. Perhaps someday—but not yet. Not for a while.

I was halfway down the stairs when an odd thing occurred to me. In all his room there had not been a single picture of Julia.

Thirteen_____

That afternoon I spent moving my things into Bobby's room. Not that it took all that long to transfer my clothing and a few personal belongings; what held things up were the constant confrontations with Bobby who was not at all receptive to having a sister for a roommate.

"You're a girl, Rae," he kept exclaiming. "My gosh, you're a girl!" And to Mother—"Rae's a girl, Mom!"

"So I've noticed," Mother said dryly, "and I can understand your feelings, but there doesn't seem to be an alternative. She can't get along in the same room with Julia, and she has to sleep somewhere."

"She could room with Peter," Bobby suggested.

"You know that's impossible. Peter would have a fit. Besides, his room has only one bed."

"Then put her in the garage," Bobby said. "Or let her go move in with her friend Carolyn."

"Rachel's your sister," Mother said, "and as difficult as she is being these days, we can't shove her off onto other people. If it's your privacy you're worried about we can hang a curtain down the center of the room to act as a partition."

So a good hour was spent in rigging up a kind of frame to hold the curtain, and another half hour at least in deciding what the curtain should consist of. We finally used a bed sheet, and by the time the room was divided to Bobby's satisfaction and he had decided which side of the closet I could have, it was almost time for dinner.

On my last trip to my old room I removed the needle from the stereo and took the photograph of Mike off the top of the bureau. Mike might not still be mine, but his picture was, and I didn't plan to leave it behind to be enjoyed by Julia. I took the posters off the walls and rolled them up and put them under one of the beds, and I took my pink dress off its hanger and wadded it up and put it in the Goodwill bag in the laundry room. My books I had to leave on the shelves because there was no place in Bob's room to put them, but I did take with me the witchcraft books which I put in a drawer with my underwear and night clothes.

Standing in the doorway, giving the room one last once over, I could not help but notice how empty it was with my own things removed from it. How little Julia had brought with her when she made the move from Pine Crest to Albuquerque! I had not really noticed this before because my own belongings had filled the room with so much clutter, but with their removal there remained almost nothing to show that the room still had an occupant.

It's funny, I thought, she doesn't even have a picture of her parents. There were no mementos or trinkets, no snapshots or scrapbooks, no favorite books or stuffed animals or wall decorations. It was as though the girl who lived here had come to us without a past, had materialized out of thin air on our doorstep with no link at all with another time or place.

The only thing that was Julia's was the letter that had come that morning, which she had tossed, unopened, onto the bureau.

Good-bye, dear old room, I thought gloomily.

If there had been a way I could have escaped the family dinner table and eaten alone in the kitchen I would have done so. I knew however that there was no sense in even bringing up the question. My parents considered the dinner hour a time for the family to be together and catch up on all the events of the day. And so I sat and poked at my food while Bobby gave Dad and Peter a full and exaggerated account of the morning's excitement, playing particular attention to his own part in the drama.

"I pushed the lawn mower down to his house," he said, "and rang the doorbell. When nobody answered I got this feeling like something terrible had happened. I don't know how I knew it, I just did. So I opened the door and there right in front of my eyes was Professor Jarvis with this rope—"

"What?" I exclaimed, jolted into speech.

"Well, not exactly a rope, but the way he was lying I couldn't tell about that. So I said, 'Professor, what happened?' And he didn't answer. So I rolled him over and listened to his heart—"

"Bob ran home and told us," Mother said, taking over the story. "It was a stroke, poor man. I guess at his age that sort of thing is to be expected, but it's still a shock when it occurs. I saw him just the other day out working in his yard and he looked so fit and healthy."

"I wish you wouldn't talk about him as though he were dead," I said. "He's not, you know. He can get well again."

"We can certainly hope so," Mother said. "After dinner I'm going to phone the hospital. There may have been some change since Mrs. Gallagher called this afternoon."

"You won't have to do that," Julia said. "I'm going to the hospital later this evening. I'll bring back a report on how the professor is doing."

"You're going to the hospital?" My heart caught in my chest. "Why should you do that?"

"Mike's driving over to pick up his mother," Julia said pleasantly, "and he asked me if I wanted to ride along."

"How nice!" Mother said. "I'll cut some flowers for you to take with you. If the professor isn't well enough to enjoy them, at least they may make the room a little less depressing for his poor daughter."

"But why should Julia go to the hospital?" I demanded. "She isn't a friend of Professor Jarvis's. She hardly knew him and besides that—besides that—" I let the sentence trail off weakly. The words I wanted to speak burned on my tongue, but I could not say them. Besides that, I longed to shout, Julia is the one responsible for his being in the hospital! Whatever purpose she has for going there has to be a bad one. She's planning something—something terrible!

Instead, with a violent effort, I brought my voice under control.

"I want to go too," I said.

I thought I saw a flicker of irritation in Julia's eyes.

"We're not going to stay," she said. "We're just going to pick up Mike's mother."

"That's all right," I replied. "I don't plan to stay long either."

"Then why do you want to go?"

Out of the blue an answer occurred to me. "I want to meet Mrs. Chavez. The professor has talked about her so often, I'd like to see her and tell her how sorry we are and find out if she needs anything while she's here."

"That's a good idea." Dad was regarding me with more approval than he'd shown for weeks. "That would be a gracious thing to do, Rae."

"And you can take her the house key," Mother said. "I locked up the Jarvis house. She and her husband will be wanting to sleep there."

"But I can do that!" There was an edge to Julia's normally well-modulated voice. "There's no reason Rachel has to come. Besides, there may not be room in the car considering we have to pick up Mrs. Gallagher."

"There's plenty of room for four people to ride in Mike's car," I said firmly. "It's not a two-seater, you know. And I'm sure he won't mind my going, if that's what you were going to bring up next. Remember, he's as fond of me as if I were his little sister."

"Don't be so high-headed, Rachel!" Real anger flashed in Julia's eyes. "You just kill your own snakes and leave me kill mine!"

"What?" I said, and from his seat beside me Bobby echoed the question, "What was that you said? About killing snakes?"

"It's just a pussy term." Julia flushed. "Somethin' they say back home. What I meant was that Rachel should mind her own business. She's not goin' with Mike no more and there's no good reason she's got to shove in where she's not wanted."

There was a moment of silence. Everyone at the table was staring at Julia as though unable to believe their ears.

It was Dad, at last, who said gently, "You can't mean that, Julie. It's not as though you and Mike were going out on a date. Rae has as much right to go over to the hospital as you do. Don't let the quarrel you girls had last night, whatever it may have been about, stand between you. We're all one family; let's try our best to get along together."

Julia dropped her eyes and swallowed hard. From where I sat across from her, I could see the tendons in her neck standing out like taut wires as she struggled to contain her emotions. For once things were not going as she wanted. For the first time since her arrival in our home she did not have the situation under control.

Why, I wasn't sure, but for some reason the last thing in the world that Julia wanted was for me to accompany her on her trip to the hospital.

"All right," she said finally in a low, tight voice. "All right, Tom. You're right, of course. I'm sorry I got so—so upset."

"Rae can be pretty upsetting sometimes," Peter said sympathetically. "I can see where you wouldn't especially want her tagging along."

"I wish you girls would make up," Bobby said. "Then Rae could move back into her own bedroom. How am I going to have guys over or anything if I've got a sister sitting in there reading her dumb books on the other side of a flowered sheet?"

"Rae can move back whenever she likes," Dad said. "I'm sure she won't find it too easy herself, rooming with an eleven-year-old brother. Nothing would make me happier than to see—"

The doorbell rang.

"That's Mike." Julia kept her eyes on the table. I wondered if she was afraid that if she lifted them she would disclose something that she did not want us to see.

"I'll get it," I said, shoving back my chair. "I'm through eating."

I jumped up quickly, before Mother could open her mouth to protest the pile of untouched food on my plate, and hurried to the door. When I pulled it open it seemed for a moment as though time had fallen away and it was spring again, for there was Mike, his thumbs hooked casually in the pockets of his jeans, his hair already fluffing up from an effort at combing that had not survived the short trip from his yard to ours. I'd opened the door to find him this way so many times, flashing his quick, happy grin, saying, "Hi, Carrot-top. Are you ready?"

Now he said, "Hello, Rae. Is Julia ready?"

"Almost," I said. "We're just finishing dinner. Is it all right if I go with you to the hospital?"

"Sure," Mike said. "Glad to have you. I know you must be worried about the professor. You were always so fond of the old guy."

"Not 'were,' " I said for the second time that evening. " 'Am.' He's alive, Mike! He's still alive!"

But a half hour later, standing with Mrs. Gallagher and Bonnie Chavez in the white-walled room at Presbyterian Hospital, I was not so certain.

"Is he—I mean, are you sure he's—breathing?" I whispered.

"Yes, dear. Do you see that gauge? It's measuring his heart beat." Mrs. Gallagher put a plump arm comfortingly around my shoulders. "He's doing as well as can be expected under the circumstances. It's just lucky that Bobby found him when he did."

"I can't believe it," Bonnie Chavez said tremulously. She was a gentle-faced woman who looked startlingly like the photograph of Mrs. Jarvis which the professor kept on the piano in his living room. "Daddy was always so strong and healthy. That's the only reason we agreed to letting him stay alone after Mother died. We wanted him to come live with us, but he was so definite about not wanting to leave Albuquerque. He had so many friends here and he loved the stimulation of being close to the University."

"Something like this could have occurred any place," Mrs. Gallagher told her. "In Clovis as well as here. You mustn't blame yourself. No one is to blame."

Oh, yes, someone is, I thought miserably.

Cautiously, so as not to risk disturbing the various tubes and tapes, I moved closer to the bed and stood, gazing down at the motionless figure which had only yesterday been a vital, active human being. The face on the pillow appeared so shrunken and strange that if it had not been for the crown of snowy hair I might not even have recognized it as the professor's. The lips hung slack over a formless cavity of mouth, and the eyes were sunken deep into dark hollows beneath the shaggy brows.

I reached out gently and touched the gnarled

hand which lay limp upon the sheet, and I felt no answering pressure, no response of any sort from the lifeless fingers.

"He looks so different," I said haltingly. "His face—"

"It's his teeth," Mrs. Gallagher said. "One of the first things they did when we got here was to take out his dentures. They were afraid they might slip and get caught in his throat while he was unconscious."

"And his glasses," Mrs. Chavez said. "We were so used to seeing him wearing glasses. And, of course, he was always smiling and talking, never still like this. Even when he was sleeping, I don't think I've ever seen him this still."

There were footsteps behind us and Bonnie Chavez turned.

"Oh, how pretty!" she exclaimed, trying to smile. "Look, Mrs. Gallagher, we have flowers!"

"Aunt Leslie thought you might enjoy them," Julia said. "Mike and I stopped at the gift shop on the way up and got a card to go with them."

"Thank you, dear. They're lovely," Mrs. Chavez said politely. "Now I must try to place you. Are you related to the kind woman who phoned me to tell me about my father's accident?"

"I'm Julia, her niece," Julia said. "And this is Mrs. Gallagher's son Mike. We all just loved your father. He was a very popular person."

"I used to do his yard work," Mike said. "He was a great guy to work for, always patient about letting me plan my work time around swim meets. He'd come and stand and talk to me while I did the edging. He was interested in so many things that he could hold a conversation about anything."

"He was wonderful with young people," Mrs. Gallagher said. "It was the professor who first got Mike started reading. When he was a little boy he hated to read, and then one day Professor Jarvis brought over a book about a boy who wanted to be a long distance swimmer, and Mike never laid it down until it was finished."

Their voices droned on behind me, rising and falling in a pattern of forced conversation, and I turned my mind from them and concentrated all the strength of my thoughts upon the figure on the bed.

Professor, I cried silently, this is Rachel, your friend! Are you there, Professor, someplace beneath the sagging skin and the deathmask face? Are you thinking and knowing? Are you *there*?

The professor did not move. His fingers remained limp in the warmth of my hand, and I tightened my grasp upon them, willing them to stir, to give me some sort of movement so that I would know life existed.

Professor, it's Rachel, I told him frantically. Please, look at me, speak to me, do *something*!

"We really have to be going," Mrs. Gallagher was saying. "Are you sure there's nothing more we can do for you? Will you be staying at your father's house?"

"Yes," Mrs. Chavez said. "We'll be going there later. My husband's gone out to get something for us to eat, and we'll sit with Daddy a bit longer. I'm sure the nurses are competent, it's just that I hate the thought of going off and leaving him with strangers."

"If you need any errands run, just let me know,"

Mike said. "My hours at the pool are pretty loose."

"Do call on me too," Julia said. "I'm free to do anything that will help. Let me know if you would like to have me come down and sit with your father a while so that you can get some rest."

It was then that I saw it, the flicker of an eyelid. If I had not had my gaze so concentrated upon the professor's face I would have missed it altogether. Now, suddenly, I saw that the shaded eyes, sunken deep into the sockets, were not closed after all. They were open and staring, half covered by the shadow of the gray lashes, and with no facial movement to accentuate them they seemed as expressionless as the eyes of a plastic doll.

Yet when I leaned closer and could see into them, they were far from empty. They were thinking, knowing eyes, and they looked straight into my own.

Save me, they screamed from the confines of the immobile face. Save me, Rachel! Get me out of here! I'm trapped! I cannot help you! You must do it alone!

"—wonderful of all of you," Bonnie Chavez was saying, her voice warm with gratitude. "It's so good to know that Daddy's friends are on call to help. It would have meant so much to him, knowing how many of his neighbors loved him and were concerned about him."

"You must let me help," Julia said. "I'd be so glad to sit with him. I lost my own father just recently and I know what it means—"

She would be so glad to sit with him. Of course. What was it I had read just yesterday—that a witch could cause death by walking three times clockwise around a sick man? The book had described this as difficult to accomplish because most beds stood against a wall.

But a hospital bed was on rollers.

Fourteen _____

I could not fall asleep that night. Not that this was unusual. How long ago it seemed since I had fallen asleep quickly and easily, the moment my head touched the pillow, and waked in the morning refreshed and happy! On this night I could not even read, for Bobby refused to let me have the light on, so I lay tense and restless in the stuffy, cramped area on the far side of the room divider, listening to the snoring sounds my brother made in slumber and trying not to be aware of the odor of his tennis shoes which lay on the floor directly on the other side of the flowered sheet.

In the room above me, the lovely, yellow walled room which I had painted myself the summer before, lay Julia. I could picture her there, lying flat and still, her hair loose upon the pillow, her lips curved slightly as she smiled in her sleep. Or was she sleeping? Perhaps, instead, she was lying awake, just as I was, thinking back upon the events of the day and planning for tomorrow.

Tomorrow—and the next day—and the day beyond that—how far ahead did Julia's planning go? If only it were possible to look through those eyes of hers into the depths of her mind! I could not believe that she was moving impulsively along one day at a time in a haphazard manner. What had happened today was for Julia one step along a road toward a particular destination. What was it Julia wanted so desperately? Where was her road leading? And what was to become of us all if and when she reached her goal?

If I could answer these questions, perhaps I would be able to stop her. But where did the answers lie? Not in the books I had brought home from the library; I had read those from cover to cover. Not in Professor Jarvis, a speechless, motionless captive in a hospital bed. If only there were someone, I thought, who knew Julia before she came here, someone who might have an understanding of her motives and intentions. But who? Her parents were dead and so was the woman who worked for them. Julia had no brothers or sisters, and she had spent so little time in Pine Crest that it was doubtful that she would have had friends there of the sort in whom she would have confided.

No family, no friends. It was like trying to make sense out of a book that began in the middle with nothing before it but blank pages. No matter how carefully one concentrated upon the present chapter, there was no way to make sense out of what was happening because there was no knowledge of what had come before.

The more I pondered the problem the more insurmountable it became, and when I fell asleep at last it was a fitful, dream-laden sleep that brought little rest.

In the dream I was running along the edge of a road. Red cliffs rose to one side and a sheer dropoff lay on the other, and Mike was running with me.

"Will we get there in time?" I cried to him. "Can we get there before it happens?"

"Are you crazy, Rae?" he shouted. "If you'd only explain—"

"I can't!" I gasped. "There's no time!"

And far ahead at the curve of the road there appeared, as I had known there would, a car. I knew who was driving, for I had had this dream before. Long before the car was close enough for me to see the face behind the wheel, I was running toward it down the middle of the road, waving and shouting.

"Stop!" I cried. "Stop!"

And then, just as had happened the last time the dream had occurred, as the car was bearing down upon me to the point where I could actually see the expression in the driver's eyes, I awoke.

There was nothing but darkness and for a moment I was not certain where I was. I was drenched with perspiration and yet I was shaking as though I were cold, cold in this stuffy little room in the middle of summer. I stretched out my hand and felt the sheet hanging by the side of the bed and remembered. It was Bobby's room, and I was here because I had chosen to be.

The horror of the dream still clung to me. I lay quiet, breathing hard, trying to collect myself. It was at that moment that a thought occurred to me, a thought that seemed to come from nowhere and had nothing whatsoever to do with my nightmare.

Julia *did* have a friend who knew her before she came to Albuquerque! The friend had written her a letter that had arrived that very morning!

How was it that I had not reacted to this sooner! My heart began to pound with excitement. If Julia had not moved it, the letter lay right now on the bureau in the room where she was sleeping. All I had to do was go upstairs and get it and any information in it was mine!

Did I dare? Even as I asked myself the question I was sitting up and swinging my legs over the side of the bed. Bobby's snores told me that he was so deeply asleep that he would not have reacted if a herd of elephants had come thundering by. I shoved aside the makeshift curtain and got out of bed and crossed the room and went down the hall to the stairs. My feet made no sound. I knew the house so well that there was no need for a light.

Once on the second floor, I glided soundlessly down the hall to the door of the room that had so recently been my own. It was not until my hand was actually on the knob that I began to feel frightened. What if Julia was not asleep?

She has to be, I told myself reassuringly. It's almost dawn! It's the time of night when people sleep the hardest! But Julia was not "people" in any ordinary sense of the word. Who could say which hours she might choose for her supernatural activities? Were spells that were cast during the hours of darkness more potent than those cast in the light of day? If so, this might be the very time when Julia was most likely to be awake.

Did I have a choice? No, I thought, none. If I was to get my hands on that letter it must be now.

Breathing a silent prayer I turned the knob and shoved open the door.

This room was not as dark as Bobby's had been, for it looked toward the east where the sky above the Sandia Mountains was beginning to lighten with the promise of a new day. I could see, very faintly, the outline of the twin beds with Julia's form upon one of them. The shape on the bed had not stirred with the opening of the door and it did not now as I put a tentative foot into the room.

Slowly and carefully, feeling ahead along the carpet with each bare foot, I crossed the room and reached the chest of drawers at the far end. In the mirror above it I could see my own image, a blob of featureless black, moving against the lesser darkness of the east window. Would the letter still be there? Yes, it was. I could make out the square white shape of the envelope against the surface of the bureau. As I was reaching out my hand to pick it up, Julia gave an odd little moaning sound and changed her position on the bed. The sheets rustled and the springs creaked, and my hand froze in midair, poised above the letter.

For a long moment I stood there absolutely motionless, afraid even to breathe. The thud of my heart seemed to fill the entire room. I could not imagine that Julia could help but hear it. Apparently she did not, however, because she did not move again, and as time passed I began to relax a little. Once again I lowered my hand, and this time it closed upon the envelope.

The trip back across the room was as torturous as the first crossing, perhaps more so, for in the short time since I had entered the sky had become lighter. Or perhaps my eyes had become more accustomed to the darkness. For whatever reason, the feeling of concealment was gone, and the sound and movement from Julia had put my nerves at the cracking point. It was with a breath of relief that I stepped through the door and eased it closed behind me.

Moving more quickly, but as silently as possible, I slipped back down the hall and stairs to the hallway below. Once there I hesitated, undecided as to what to do next. I needed a reading light, something I would not have if I returned to Bobby's bedroom. I was still too worried about detection to feel safe in turning on any of the lights in the downstairs living area. Finally I thought of the bathroom. I went inside and closed the door and pushed in the button in the center of the knob. At the reassuring click of the lock falling into place my knees went suddenly weak from release of tension. I flicked on the light and sank down gratefully on the edge of the tub.

I sat there a moment, letting my heart slow down, blinking my eyes to accustom them to the burst of brilliance. Then I turned my attention to the letter. I was surprised to see that it was still unopened.

How could she? I thought. It's the first letter she's received from anybody since she arrived here. I should have thought she would have been so glad to hear from one of her friends that she would have ripped it open at once.

How short a time ago it was that I would have recoiled in horror at the thought of opening a letter addressed to someone else! Now I did not even pause. Quickly I ran my thumb under the flap of the envelope and pulled it open.

The stationery was cute and informal, of the type that comes in multicolored pads with matching envelopes. At the top of the sheet in black block letters was printed "Memos From Mary."

Mary's handwriting was round and even and slanted slightly upward as it ran across the page. The letter was a short one:

> Dear Julie—
>   How is your summer going? How come I haven't heard from you about the house party? Will your mother and dad let you come? I do hope so! Without you and your guitar and silly jokes and all it just won't be fun for anybody. I got a note from Gail and she can make it and so can Sharon and Tippy. Remember, it's the third week in August and we can all go back to school together from here.
>   My brother Dick saw your picture in the yearbook and he wants to be the one to meet your plane! Write soon and tell me that you can make it for sure.
>
> Love,
> *Mary*

That was all.

All.

My disappointment was so acute that I actually felt physically ill. For this I had hoped and schemed and frightened myself to death sneaking into Julia's bedroom, for this plain, ordinary, dull little note. Julia was invited to a house party and had evidently been planning to clear the matter with her parents. Of course, she had had no chance to do so. In all the turmoil of the accident and the subsequent move to Albuquerque she had undoubtedly forgotten all about something as trivial as a schoolmate's party at the end of vacation.

What did the letter tell me about Julia? Absolutely nothing. In fact, it was hard to visualize Julia as the person to whom such a note might be written. A Julia who told "silly jokes" and planned get-togethers with girl friends was a far cry from the intense, plotting, calculating Julia who killed a little dog with a wax statue and put a kind old man in the hospital. And both of these were different from the Julia who put a motherly arm around Bobby when he was upset, who gave my mother a daughterly hand in the kitchen, who smiled up lovingly at my father and called him "Tom." Was there really one girl named Julia, a definite and distinct personality, or were there a dozen Julias, all of them different?

Was Mary, as Julia's friend and possibly even her roommate, aware of her supernatural talents? Would it be possible for her to have spent a couple of years living closely with Julia in the confines of a private boarding school, to have formed a close enough relationship so that a party "just won't be fun for anybody" without Julia there, and not know that she was different from other people?

No, it wasn't, I told myself. Mary must know a lot of things that she had no reason to refer to in this letter. If only I knew her, I thought helplessly. If I could just sit down and talk with her for a little while! I could ask about Julia's relationship with her parents and what other students thought of her and what subject she was interested in. I could find out if there were any strange happenings, collapses and illnesses and cases of hives, among the student body while Julia was with them. I might even find out what it was Julia wanted, where she was headed. Girls who live closely together find out such things about each other rather quickly. They have to talk about *something* during the evenings when they are finished with studying and it isn't yet time to go to bed. If I could talk with her—

Why not? The question came into my mind like a kind of explosion. Why don't you talk with Mary Carncross? Haven't you ever heard of an invention called a telephone?

Call her long distance? Ask her all my questions? Why in the world shouldn't I? The one catch would be making the call with enough privacy so that I could talk freely. There were two telephone extensions in our home, one in the downstairs hallway and the other in the kitchen, and both were directly in the line of family traffic. I could almost count on the fact that any time of the day or evening I settled down to make a phone call enough family members would come wandering through so that the nature of my conversation was public knowledge.

The call would have to be made from some place outside our home unless—

And here again a solution leapt fullblown into my mind. *Unless I made the call right now!* The family was sleeping and would remain that way for at least another hour. I glanced at my watch. Five forty-five. There was a two-hour time difference between Albuquerque and the East Coast.

That meant that in Boston it would be seven-forty-five, a little early for a call but not out of the question.

I'll do it, I decided. It may not get me anywhere, but there's nothing to lose by trying. At least, it's better than sitting here doing nothing.

I decided to call from the kitchen since it was farther from the bedrooms than the extension in the hallway. There was also a door that I could close to muffle the sound of my voice. I got up from the edge of the bathtub and turned out the light and let myself out into the hallway. The house was no longer dark but gray and still with the pale half-light of dawn. I went soundlessly down the empty hall to the kitchen and pulled shut the door and took the telephone receiver off the hook. I dialed the operator, squinting to make out the information in the upper left-hand corner of Mary Carncross's envelope.

"I need a number," I said. "I want to call the Carncross residence in Boston, Massachusetts. I don't have the first name, but the address is 1572 Jackson Avenue."

"Just a moment, please," the operator said in a singsong voice. "I'll contact information."

There were a number of clicks and buzzes, and then a second voice came on, sounding strange and far away as though it were coming from another land. The two operators conversed for a moment and there was another click and silence.

Then, at the far end of the line, a phone began to ring. I clutched the receiver hard against my ear and was surprised to find that my hand was shaking.

"Hello?" a woman's voice said. "Hello?"

"Hello." My own voice came out unnaturally high and nervous. I tried to haul it down into a more normal tone. "Could I please speak to Mary?"

"She's asleep," the woman said. "This is too early to be calling her."

"I know," I said. "I'm sorry. I'm calling from Albuquerque, New Mexico. It's about the house party."

"Oh." The woman sounded slightly less irritated. "Well, in that case I'll wake her. I know she's been going crazy trying to get together with everybody. Just a moment, please."

There was a wait that seemed to go on forever and then a girl's voice, still dull with sleep, came on the line and said, "Hello. This is Mary."

"Mary—" and now suddenly I did not know what to say. "I'm Rachel Bryant. My cousin Julia Grant is one of your classmates at boarding school."

"You're Julie's cousin? From Pine Crest?"

"No," I said. "From Albuquerque, New Mexico. There was a terrible accident back the beginning of June right after Julia got home for summer vacation. Both her parents were killed in an automobile wreck. Julia has come to live with us."

"Her parents were killed?" The drowsiness was gone from the girl's voice now. She sounded wide awake and sincerely distressed. "How awful! Why, they were such a close family! Julie just adored her parents, especially her mother! The poor thing! Can I talk to her?"

"No," I said quickly. "She can't—I mean, she's so broken up she can't face talking about it. Besides, she's in bed right now. I'm calling because of your

letter. It came yesterday. Julia had forgotten all
about the party and I told her I'd call for her—to
apologize to you for her not having written."

"Oh, tell her I understand," Mary said with such
sincerity that I felt guilty about the deception.
"Who could think about a party after a tragedy
like that! Please tell her how bad I feel for her, and
the other girls will too when they hear. Julie's
everybody's favorite person. She is coming back to
school in the fall, isn't she?"

"I don't know," I said. "It hasn't been decided
yet."

"She just has to," Mary said. "It won't be the
same if she's not there. Julie's the spark plug for
everything. She's class president and lead soprano
in the choir and she's in charge of the talent day
program and—oh, there's just no way any of us can
go through senior year without Julie."

"The choir?" I said, startled. "Julia sings in a
choir?"

"In chapel every Sunday and at the Wednesday
evening worship service. You know what a beautiful voice she has. How is she taking it? Is she
holding up all right?"

"She's adjusting well," I said. "She's bearing up
much better than anybody would have thought."

It was in my mind, the question I wanted to ask
her. I could not bring it to my lips. Now that I
actually had Mary Carncross on the telephone and
had heard the very real concern and affection in
her voice when she spoke of Julia, how could I ask
it? How could I say, "Has anything ever occurred
that has led you to believe that this dear friend of
yours might be a practicing witch?"

I grasped instead for something less dramatic.

"Does Julia," I asked, "like dogs?"

"Does she what?"

"Like dogs? Any kind of dogs?"

"I don't know," Mary said blankly. "I guess so. Doesn't everybody?"

"Did you ever see her pet one?"

"No," Mary said. "Not at school. We weren't permitted to keep pets in the dormitory." She sounded bewildered. "Why did you ask that?"

The conversation was taking me nowhere. Worse than that, Mary was beginning to become suspicious. I had put through my phone call impulsively without having properly planned it, and as a result I was floundering. My precious opportunity was being wasted and it would not come again.

"Who did you say this was?" Mary Carncross asked. "Are you really a cousin of Julie's? Are you sure this is a long distance call? You're not just somebody playing a joke?"

There was no help for it. I must plunge ahead or the chance would be lost forever.

"Do you know," I asked, "if Julia ever made a study of witchcraft?"

There was a long pause. When Mary finally spoke again, her voice was clipped and cold.

"I don't know what kind of kook you are," she said shortly, "or why you decided to call me, but you'd better not make any accusations about Julie Grant. I've been her roommate for two years and I know her backwards and forwards. She's as clean and straight and open as sunshine. You're either a troublemaker out to hurt her, or you're just plain crazy."

Fifteen _____

"Just plain crazy"? Was I? My suspicions would seem so to many people. Mary Carncross thought Julia one of the finest people in the world. It was not as though she didn't know her either, for as her roommate of two years she should know her better than I. Was it possible that anyone as evil as the Julia I knew—or thought I knew—could keep up a pretext that long? Would Mary Carncross lie to protect her? If so, why?

Am I crazy? I asked myself. I could not believe that I was. I was on the edge of something crazy, perhaps, but I myself was sane. I knew the things that Julia had done. I had not invented them. The professor understood, I could tell that by his eyes. The fear there last night had not been imagined. Something terrible was happening one step at a time, and the fact that I had no proof to offer did not make it any the less real.

What should I do now?

An immediate answer occurred to me, one thing

that must be done before any other, and I did it. Still by the telephone, I looked up the number of the Presbyterian Hospital and dialed it.

"Hello," I said. "I am calling to tell you that the life of your patient Professor Jarvis has been threatened. If you have any regard for his safety you will restrict all visitors to members of his immediate family."

Not waiting for a response, I replaced the receiver on the hook. I could imagine the reaction at the front desk of the hospital office. Would the plump woman I had seen there the night before still be on duty? If so, she had probably fainted on top of the visitors' register. Or perhaps a replacement had taken over her position by this time, someone who had never heard of Professor Jarvis. She would now be flipping frantically through the book of patients, trying to place him. Now she would have found him. She would be lifting the receiver—dialing someone with authority.

"I've had the most disturbing call," she might be saying. "A murder threat to one of our patients!"

So much for that, I thought with a feeling of satisfaction. Julia would not have a chance to walk three times clockwise around that particular bed.

But in making the call I had cut off my own contact with the professor as well as Julia's. That contact might have been extremely helpful. The night before, in my final moment at the hospital, I had come to realize that it was possible to communicate with Professor Jarvis. His eyes had been intelligent and alive, receptive to such communication. I might have presented him with questions and worked up some sort of code between us—a blink of the eyes once for yes, twice for no. "Spell out your answer, Professor," I might have told him. "One blink for A, two for B, three for C." It might have taken us hours to have gotten across one short message, but it could have been well worth the effort. The knowledge that lay buried in that snow white head was invaluable. If we had been able to have spoken to each other for even one moment, I was sure he could have steered me to an answer. He could have given me enough information about the workings of witchcraft so that I could have exposed Julia for what she was.

But this was not to be. Given the choice, his safety was more important than the help he might give me. Somehow I must work out a solution by myself. I had a number of pieces to the puzzle, but they would not fit together. The Julia I knew and the Julie known by Mary Carncross appeared on the surface to be two entirely different people. Her Julie went to church and sang lead soprano with the choir. This seemed impossible. Could anyone practice black magic and still be a participating member of a Christian church? As far as I could recall we had not attended church since Julia had come to live with us. My own family was lax about going, ever since Pete and I had become teenagers and our lives had filled with too many conflicting activities. And Julia herself had never suggested going to church. As far as the singing went, I had never heard Julia sing. She had not brought a guitar home with her, unless it was crammed somehow into one of those boxes stored in the attic.

And the Julie of the "silly jokes"—to me she did not exist. There was no levity, no sense of fun in the Julia I knew. Could it exist beneath the surface, I asked myself. Could it have lain hidden for these past months, buried beneath the weight of parental loss?

No—no. I could not believe that to be the case.

Nothing fit—nothing fit. I had to have more information.

I need more to go on, I thought hopelessly. I need something that makes all the parts go together into some kind of workable whole. With Professor Jarvis no longer able to help me, where could I turn? Only to the books, both of which I had read through several times.

Perhaps I'm missing something, I thought. I'll go back and read them again.

Leaving the kitchen I went softly down the hall and let myself back into Bobby's bedroom. He was sleeping as deeply as he had been when I had left him. In the time since I had been gone the room had grown light enough so that reading was possible.

I opened the drawer in which I had stored the books and took them out and carried them over to the bed.

The history book looked solid and factual and unhelpful. There was nothing factual about the type of information for which I was searching. I was looking for a will-o'-the-wisp, a flickering light, a glimpse past the solid and the real into another kind of reality. It was like trying to grasp quicksilver.

I shoved that book aside and picked up the second, the one on superstitions. This was where I would start and somewhere, somewhere, in these pages, I would find something I could work on.

That "something" turned out to be on page

seventy-three: "There is a superstition, widely held
among believers in magic, that a witch cannot be
photographed." I read over the statement once,
stopped, and read it again. It was followed by a
series of stories supposedly gleaned from interviews with old-time residents of the backwoods
area of the Ozarks. They all concerned attempts
that had been made to photograph women who
practiced the art of witchcraft.

One told about a tourist who was driving
through the Ozarks and saw an old woman leading
a cow down a country road. She was so picturesque
that the tourist had stopped his car and despite
the woman's protests had snapped her picture with
his Instamatic. Arriving home, he had taken his
film to be developed at a drugstore. The prints he
got back included one of a cow walking alone
along a road. The lead rope stuck straight out in
front and ended in midair. The woman was nowhere in the picture.

There was another story about a national magazine that had sent a writer-photographer team
back into the hills to do an article on present-day
witchcraft. The writer had interviewed a number
of women who claimed to be witches and the photographer had taken their pictures. When the photographs were printed, several of them contained
no people.

The author of the book called these "tales from
the hills." "These are the sorts of stories that run
from generation to generation," he wrote,

> growing stranger with each telling. Over the
> years the names of the people involved be-
> come lost or are replaced by other names. No

one can offer any proof of their credibility. At the same time, they are accepted by a large number of older people and a surprising number of younger ones who have learned them from their parents. As short a time as three years before this book is being written a coed at a southeastern college refused to have her picture taken for the school yearbook. Her reason, confessed finally to her counselor, was that "witchcraft runs in our family" and she did not want this revealed to her classmates by having the frame turn out empty.

It was not a large section of the book, only a couple of paragraphs, but it was enough to start my heart beating wildly. How was it that I had bypassed this before? In my rush to find more applicable material I had skipped over a section that was in reality the most important thing in the book. It explained so much that I had found unanswerable. It explained, for instance, why it was that Mike had no picture of Julia on his bureau. She had never given him one because she didn't have one! It answered also the question of why Julia had no driver's license. I had wondered about that because at seventeen she was certainly old enough to have one. I had chalked it up to the fact that away at school as much as she was without access to a car she had had no chance to learn to drive. Now I had a better answer. To receive a license you had to have your picture taken!

What better proof could there be of Julia's status as a witch than a photograph taken of her in which she did not appear! And with my own mother a photographer, how simple it would be to have one taken! There was no way Julia could explain it. It could not be blamed on the processing, for Mother did her own. Nor could it be blamed on the camera which was a piece of expensive, professional equipment. If the situation were not so serious I might almost have laughed at the vision of Mother standing in the darkroom, surveying her roll of negatives, her brows raised, her forehead wrinkled in bewilderment.

"What in the world could have happened!" she would exclaim. "It's impossible! I know that Julia was sitting right there in that lawn chair!"

Quite suddenly, at the peak of my exuberance, I felt limp with exhaustion. Just the realization that I was finally headed somewhere definite was enough to release the tension I had been under for so long. No longer was I floundering blindly about. I had a plan—something to go on. I laid the book aside and let myself sink back upon my pillow and then, surprisingly, I fell asleep. It was a sleep of such utter weariness, so deep and so intense, that I did not wake for hours and then only because Mother came in and shook me.

"Rae?" she said worriedly. "Are you all right, dear? It's past noon!"

"Okay," I mumbled. "Okay." Mother's voice and my own seemed to come from far away. Dream voices.

"Rachel," Mother said, "open your eyes. I want to see that you're alive in there. I've never known you to sleep this long unless you're sick."

With an effort I forced my eyes open and focussed them upon her face.

"I'm okay," I said, my voice still blurred with sleep. "I just was awake a lot during the night."

"Worrying over the professor, I imagine." Mother nodded sympathetically. "I know how you feel. The first thing I did when I got up this morning was call the hospital. I think his condition must have worsened, because they've stopped allowing visitors. I had been planning to go down there at lunch time and sit with him a while so the Chavezes could go out to eat."

"Did they say he was worse?" I asked, alarmed.

"No. They just said the ruling about visitors was changed. But I can't think of any other reason. It's such a sad thing. I was wondering—" She let the sentence fade off.

"What?"

"Oh, I shouldn't even suggest it, I've got so much work to do. I've got to print up a batch of classroom shots for *Teacher* to illustrate that piece they're running on the first graders who built a doll house, and there's a dating article for *American Girl* I haven't even started on. They want a boy and girl smiling into each other's eyes and I haven't even located models. It's just that we're all so depressed a break might do us good."

"What sort of break?" I asked.

"I was thinking about a trip to Santa Fe. I could call it a business trip because I do need to stop at the Department of Development and discuss some illustrations I'm doing for an article for *New Mexico Magazine*. But that wouldn't take long, and we could go to lunch at the La Fonda and do some shopping on the plaza. On the way back there's a place I'd like to stop. There's something there I might buy for you, if you decide you like the look of it."

"It sounds nice," I said. "We haven't done any-

thing like that for a long time. We used to do so
many things together." Before Julia came, I almost
added. But I didn't.

"Would you like to plan it for tomorrow?"
Mother asked me. "I could phone the editor at
New Mexico Magazine and set up an appointment.
I could take the *American Girl* pictures this after-
noon if you and Mike would pose for them, and
you could help me with the printing tonight."

"I don't want to pose with Mike," I said, sitting
up in bed. My body felt numb from having lain
so long in one position. "You know we aren't going
together anymore."

"What difference does that make?" Mother
asked. "You're still friends, aren't you? And I can't
use you with Peter. You look too much like brother
and sister."

"Use Julia," I said. How easy it was! I couldn't
have planned the situation better if I had invented
it from scratch. "Let Julia pose with Mike. You've
talked about wanting to photograph her."

Mother frowned thoughtfully. "I don't know.
She looks—"

"Looks what?"

"I don't know exactly—just not quite right for
the picture. She's lovely looking, of course, but too
old."

"How can she be too old?" I asked, surprised.
"She's seventeen, the same age as Mike."

"That's true. It's just that there's something
about her face that seems older than her years.
Her eyes, maybe, or her mouth." Mother seemed as
confused as I was over the statement. "I never
thought about it until now, picturing the way she
would look in a photograph. I just have this feel-

ing she might come across too old for *American Girl*."

"I think she'd look fine," I said. "Her dark coloring would be a good contrast to Mike's blondness. She could wear something springtimish—like that pink dress I made."

"Well—maybe. That dress was pretty on her."

"Think how soulfully she and Mike could look at each other," I said, trying to keep the irony from my voice. "They wouldn't even have to act. It would be natural."

"There's that, of course. Okay, you've convinced me." Mother accepted the idea. "There won't be any problem getting them together. Mike's out in the living room right now, and Julia was just asking if she could help me with anything. I'll march them out into the backyard and go to it. I'd like to get them with leaf shadows across their faces."

"She might not want to do it," I said. "She might be shy."

"She'll get over that," Mother said. "Anybody in this family has to be prepared to act as a model when needed. You know that—it's a rule of the house!"

She left the room, and I got up and got dressed and made the bed and let a little time go past as I washed my face and did my eyes and fooled around with my hair. When I left the bedroom at last I did not go outside but went instead up the stairs and into my room which was now Julia's and over to the window where I could see down into the backyard. They were out there. Mother had her camera on a tripod, and Mike and Julia were standing together over by the elm tree. I could not see Julia's face but I could tell by the rigidity of her stance that she was not happy with the situation.

I almost laughed out loud.

So much for you, Cousin Julia, I thought joyfully. You're caught at last! Now all I have to do is wait until Mother develops the film and then show her the paragraph I read last night.

I could see the words, sharp and black in my mind's eye, as clearly as though they were on the printed page: "There is a superstition, widely held among believers in magic, that a witch cannot be photographed."

The laughter stayed with me, joyous and triumphant, until I was halfway down the stairs when there leapt into my mind another paragraph I had recently read. It was in Mary Carncross's letter:

"My brother Dick saw your picture in the yearbook and he wants to be the one to meet your plane!"

Sixteen_____

It was all downhill the rest of the day.

Of course, there wasn't much of the rest of the day left. I went into the kitchen to get something to eat to represent breakfast and lunch combined, but my stomach was so knotted up that I couldn't face the sight or smell of food. Nor could I force myself to go into the backyard to watch the picture taking. If I could I would have gone to my room and thrown myself across the bed to weep, but I had no room to which to go. The moment I had emerged from my new sleeping area, Bobby and two of his friends had gone in to work on model planes.

So I made myself a glass of ice tea and sat down at the kitchen table and let the sick disappointment sweep over me. There was nowhere left to go either physically or mentally. All the doors were closed.

It had all seemed so perfect! For the first time that summer everything had seemed to fall into place! I had been so sure that at last I had an answer, a method of exposing Julia for her true self! Now the memory of one short sentence in a letter from a girl I didn't even know had ruined everything. There was no way I could get past it—if Mary Carncross's brother had seen Julia's picture in a school yearbook, then Julia could be photographed.

The pictures Mother was now taking would turn out. More than that, they would probably be beautiful. Did this prove that I was wrong all along, that Julia was a perfectly normal seventeen-year-old girl whom I had horribly misjudged?

No, I thought. It didn't prove that. The book had not stated that witches could not be photographed, only that there was such a superstition. The very word "superstition" implied a belief in something that was not true. The more I thought about it, the more I came to realize that I had been carried away and in a surge of desperation had jumped to an illogical assumption. Professor Jarvis, in his description of witchcraft, had never suggested that there was magic involved in the sense that there was in children's fairy tales. His explanation had accentuated the more scientific explanation of witchcraft as the utilization of the mind force to make things occur as desired. Beyond this, he had not gone. And there could be no scientific explanation for the belief that a witch could not be captured by a camera.

So now I was back where I had started, further back, really, because then at least I had had the will to struggle to find a solution. Now, after the rise of hope and the crushing defeat, I felt too emotionally exhausted to attempt another move.

Let her go, I thought wearily. Let her do what she wants to do. Nothing she does now can be any worse than the things she has already done. And yet there was the professor. I could not accept defeat and leave him forever in his present state. Could I bargain with Julia, perhaps? What was it she wanted? If I knew, I might be able to make her an offer in exchange for the professor's release. But what did I have to offer her? She already had everything—a place in our family, an inheritance from her parents, a boyfriend—two, in fact, if you included Peter—a wonderful best friend, Carolyn, and now, for all I knew, a budding career as a magazine model.

I drank my ice tea and stared at the table top. Outside the kitchen window summer was at its glorious peak. The sky rose blue and clear and cloudless beyond the rose covered fence and hummingbirds whirred dreamily about on the far side of the window screen and the sunlight splashed heavy and golden across the table and turned my tea glass to amber.

The longer I sat the more upset I became.

After a while Mother came through the kitchen carrying two rolls of newly exposed film.

"Goodness," she exclaimed, "are you just sitting here doing nothing?"

"What does it look like?" I said shortly. "Is there a law against doing nothing?" The words came out snappish and horrid, and I saw Mother wince as though she had been slapped, and I didn't care. At this point I didn't care about anything.

"There's no law," Mother said, "but, my gosh, Rae, you slept all morning and you know I'm trying to get caught up on my work so we can go to

Santa Fe tomorrow. You might have stirred yourself to do something around the place like washing the breakfast dishes."

"I didn't eat breakfast," I said. "Why should I do the dishes? Why can't wonderful Julia do them?"

"She can," Mother said, "and she's going to, bless her. And as for you, you can come along to the darkroom and help me with the printing of the doll house story. I want to get those pictures into the mail first thing in the morning and I need to be able to get them spotted tonight."

"What fun," I said, but I got up and followed her out to the garage and into the little room where she spent so many hours of her time.

I had started helping her with her printing when I was twelve and we now had a routine so well established that we never even bumped into each other in the darkness. As we entered the room Mother dropped the film she was carrying into the "hold" box, marked a wall pad with the notation "J & M or AM. GRL." and started rummaging through her negatives for the doll house series. I mixed fresh developer in one of the flat plastic trays, dumped out the smaller tray of stop bath, which had turned the color of wine from having sat too long, and refilled it, being careful not to splash any of that particular chemical on my skin. I had done that on several former occasions and found it painful.

"Okay?" Mother asked. "Ready to have the lights off?"

"Yes," I said. She flicked the switch by the door and the room went into a darkness slightly relieved by the yellow safe-lights which sent out enough of a glow to function by but would not wreck the photographic paper. I took my position at the chemical trays and Mother at the enlarger. She inserted a negative and began to sharpen the focus. When she had it right she clocked off the enlarger light and put a sheet of paper into an eight-by-ten holder and pushed the button to expose it. Her hands danced about for a few seconds, shading some areas, directing more intense light onto others. Then she took the paper out of the holder and handed it to me. I put it into the developer tray and stood, agitating it gently, while the picture began gradually to appear upon the paper. When it had developed to the right degree I lifted it with tongs and dropped it into the stop bath, which kept it from continuing to grow darker, and then into the rapid fixer which would secure the image so that it would not fade.

At first we worked in a strained sort of silence. Then, gradually, as I moved through the steps of the long familiar process, I felt my tension beginning to fade. The little room became a world of its own with Mother and me the only occupants. The years seemed to slide backward, and I could remember what it had been like to be twelve and happy.

Mother handed me another picture to run through, and as I took it from her our hands touched.

"I'm sorry," I said. "I shouldn't have been so rude there in the kitchen. You were right. I should have done the dishes."

"It wasn't that," Mother said. "I mean, the dishes aren't that important. It's just—Rachel, what is it that's happening between us—all of us? You seem so angry all the time, so apart from us. Are you jealous of Julia?"

"No," I said. "No."

"Then what?"

"I've tried to tell you," I said. "Over and over again, I've tried to make you listen, and none of you will. I thought for a while I was going to be able to prove it, to *make* you listen, and then I found I couldn't after all. I was frustrated, and I took it out on you, that's all. I said, I'm sorry."

There was a moment's silence as Mother changed negatives. Then she said, "I told you there's something I want to get you in Santa Fe tomorrow. I think it will make you happy. It may make a difference in the way you feel about things."

"I don't need a present," I said.

"You tell me when you see it. If you don't want it, then we won't get it."

"All right."

"We should start early," Mother said. "It's an hour's drive, and my appointment with the editor is for ten. That means we can do a little shopping before lunch and afterward we can drive up to the outdoor opera house. I'm sure Julia's never seen anything like it, and the mountains around Santa Fe are so totally different from the Ozarks."

I froze, the tongs in my hand, a picture held in the air halfway between two trays. My voice came out in a kind of croak.

"Julia's coming with us?"

"Why, certainly. She's very excited about it."

"But you said—" Slowly I lowered the photograph into the proper tray, trying to keep my voice steady. "You said it would be us, just you and me. That it would do us good because we were so upset about the professor."

"I never said we wouldn't take Julia. Why, honey, she's as upset as we are! She may not have known him long, but she evidently formed a very strong attachment during the few conversations they had. Besides, she's never been in Santa Fe. She'll love seeing Canyon Road and some of the other wonderful places."

"If Julia's going," I said, "then I'm staying home."

"Rachel, don't be ridiculous!" Mother exclaimed in exasperation.

"I mean it. I'm not going to spend a day cooped up in the car with Julia, no matter where we're going. That's why I moved out of the bedroom, because I couldn't bear to be with her. You know that."

"I thought that a day together doing something pleasant might draw you girls closer," Mother said. "Rae, please try. Make an effort to be gracious and loving. Julia is such a fine young person—"

"Julia's a witch!" I cried. "A witch! Can't you see it? Can't any of you see past your own noses?" I slammed the tongs down onto the edge of the tray and turned to face my mother. I could not see her face clearly in the dim light. I did not have to see it. I knew how she looked when she was upset, her mouth held tight to keep it from trembling, the freckles standing out like dark splotches against her pale face.

"She put a spell on Professor Jarvis!" I told her. "He didn't have a stroke, or if he did, it was Julia who made him have one! He knew she was a witch and he was going to talk to you about it!

Julia was afraid you would listen to him and so she put him out of the way!"

It was a last frantic try and it did not work. Could I really have thought that it would? Was there any reason that Mother would listen now to what she would not hear before? And yet, for an instant, I had thought she might. In this little room where we had worked so closely together on so many occasions, where we had held conferences and shared our thoughts and feelings, it had seemed just faintly possible that we could find each other again.

But that was not to be.

"I think you'd better go," she said.

"Go? Where?"

"Back in the house. Out in the yard. I don't care where, as long as it's someplace where I won't have to listen to crazy accusations about my sister's child. I don't care whether you like your cousin or not, Rae; you can learn to get along with her regardless. I loved your Aunt Marge very much, and Julia is all that's left of her, and it tears me to shreds to hear you slander her so cruelly."

"But, Mother—" I began miserably.

"Please, no more!" She was turned away from me now and I could tell by her voice that she was trying not to cry. "Just go along, Rae, please. I can finish the printing by myself."

"All right," I said.

I waited until she put the paper into a light-proof container and then I opened the door and stepped out into the garage. I pushed the door closed behind me and stood there wondering what to do next. Then, because there was nowhere else to go, I went into the house.

The kitchen smelled of roasting chickens. Julia had evidently started dinner. From the voices in the den I knew that Dad and Peter were both home from work and that Julia was with them. From the far end of the hall I could hear Bobby and the other airplane-makers going strong in the back bedroom; somebody was yelling something about "revving up the engine."

I went to the den and stood in the doorway. Julia was sitting on the floor in front of the coffee table on which there was spread a road map of New Mexico. Dad and Peter were sitting across from her on the sofa, and Dad was explaining, "You take the freeway here and go north. It's only sixty miles or so on a nice double-lane highway. About twenty miles north of Albuquerque there's an Indian pueblo which your Aunt Leslie will probably want to take you through. Then up here, on the outskirts of Santa Fe, you'll get into the area of the red clay cliffs. It's pretty striking scenery."

"The open air opera house is here in these mountains," Peter said, touching the map. "They'll probably be rehearsing while you're up there. Do you like opera?"

"I've never heard any," Julia said. "I don't know much about singing."

"We'll have to go sometime. I'll check and see what's planned for the rest of the season. Knowing Mom, she'll take you to eat at La Fonda, that's her and Rae's favorite place for Mexican food."

"It all sounds lovely," Julia said, tracing the route with her forefinger. "Did you say the cliffs are in this area?"

"Right here," Pete said. "I wish I were going

with you. Rae's lucky not to have a summer job; she gets to loaf around and go along on everything."

Julia moved her finger slowly up and down the black line that represented the road to Santa Fe.

"Is it all right if I take the map to my room?" she asked. "I'd like to study it a while tonight. I'm ashamed at how little I know about my adopted state."

"Go right ahead," Dad said warmly. "Keep it as long as you want to. I'm glad you're interested."

"Thanks, Tom." Julia smiled at him. It was a nice smile, gentle and gay and loving. Despite the difference in their coloring and features, when Julia smiled at my father that way she reminded me startlingly of Mother.

That night we ate chicken and rice and peas for dinner. Mother did not speak to me at the table except to ask me to pass Bobby the peas because he hadn't taken any first time around. I cleared the table and did the kitchen without being asked. Mike stopped over for a while; he had the next day off and wanted to know if Julia wanted to go on a picnic, but she told him she already had plans. After Mike left Bobby asked Julia if she wanted to play dominos, and the two of them had a game. Then Peter decided he wanted to play, so he joined them. Dad read the paper and then got some papers out of his briefcase and went over them with a red pen making little marks and corrections. Mother spotted the doll house prints and got them ready for mailing. She also remarked to Julia that she would develop the *American Girl* photos after her return from Santa Fe. I read a magazine.

It wasn't an unusual evening in any way. The
only reason I remember it in such detail is that it
was to be the last evening we were all together. It
was the evening before the end.

Seventeen

I did not get up the next morning until after Mother had gone. She had not mentioned to the family the fact that I was not going on the Santa Fe outing, and I knew it was because she hoped that I would change my mind. I was too tired of conflict to be able to face any more of it, so I remained in bed until I was certain that she and Julia had left, and then I got up and put on my shorts and a T-shirt and went out to the kitchen.

Bobby was there, eating a piece of chocolate cake.

"Is that your breakfast?" I asked him.

"It's my breakfast dessert," he said. "I had cereal already. How come you're home? I thought you were going with Mother."

"I was," I said, "but I changed my mind."

"That's dumb," Bobby said. "It means Mother doesn't have any company."

"What do you mean?" I asked. "She has Julia, doesn't she?"

"Julia's sick." Bobby took a huge forkful of cake and stuffed it into his mouth and continued to talk through a ring of chocolate icing. "Her stomach was upset and she had a headache. Mother said it sounded like she was coming down with flu."

"You mean she didn't go?" The twist in circumstances was more than I could bear. I would not have had to share the day with Julia after all! It could have been just Mother and me as I had originally anticipated!

"Mother said for her to take aspirin and stay in bed," Bobby told me. "She couldn't stay home herself because she had an appointment with an editor, but she said she'd come straight back when that was over and if Julia wasn't feeling better she'd take her to Dr. Morgan."

"It's funny Julia can't cure herself," I said.

"Huh?"

"Oh, nothing."

I went to the telephone and dialed the hospital and asked about Professor Jarvis. They transferred the call to the nurse on his floor who told me there was "no change." Then I got a piece of cake about half the size of Bobby's and sat at the kitchen table to eat it while leafing through the morning paper.

The doorbell rang announcing the arrival of a gang of Bobby's friends. They came trooping in, yelling and jabbing at each other and romping around. The noise seemed to fill the house. If anybody had been sick but Julia I would have told them to be quiet. As it was I kept my mouth shut.

I knew though that I couldn't remain in the house with all that racket. It was more than my nerves could stand. I decided that I would develop the film that Mother had left in the "hold" box so that when she got home it would be ready to be printed. It was a small way of saying "I'm sorry" for having made her unhappy.

I think back sometimes on that decision, how casually I made it. I might just as easily have decided to do something else. If that had been the case—but there is no reason to dwell upon that. As it happened, I did make the decision, and I went out to the darkroom, and there was Julia. The overhead light was on, and she was standing in front of the "hold" box with a roll of film in her hands.

"What are you doing here?" I said. "I thought you were sick!"

Her back was toward the door and evidently she had been too deeply involved in what she was doing to hear me open it, for she started and whirled to face me. The film spool dropped from her hands and rolled across the floor, leaving in its trail a long strip of undeveloped film.

I looked down at the film and up at Julia.

"You've ruined it!" I exclaimed. "You must know it can't be exposed to light!"

Julia's voice was very low and choked with fury. "You were supposed to have gone to Santa Fe with your mother!"

"Well, I didn't," I said. "And it's a good thing too or you would have wrecked all of Mother's last batch of pictures. What are you doing, trying to develop them? Don't you know that has to be done in the dark?"

"Really?" Julia said. And slowly, very deliberately, she took a second roll of film out of the box, tore off the label that held it together, and lifted it high above her head, letting the strip unwind to its full length so that the spool fell out onto the floor with a sharp, metallic clink.

I was so surprised that I did not move to stop her. I simply stood there, staring at her in amazement.

"What—" I stammered. "Why—"

"I think you know."

"I don't know at all!"

"Those books you got from the library must have told you something. If they didn't, then the professor did. It was you who suggested to your mother that she use me for a model. You did it for a reason. You wanted to show your parents that my image would not appear on the negatives."

"But it would have!" I said. "I was wrong!"

"You weren't wrong."

"But I had to have been! You've been photographed before! Mary Carncross showed your yearbook picture to her brother! You were photographed for that."

I paused. The thing that was beginning to occur to me was so incredible that I could not believe it possible, and yet—and yet—

"Julia Grant was photographed for that," I said slowly.

"Yes?"

"If a witch cannot be photographed, Julia Grant was not a witch. So you—"

"Yes?" Julia's dark eyes were fastened to my face. She smiled slightly. "Go on, Rachel. 'So you—?'"

"You are a witch," I said. "So you—*cannot be Julia Grant!*"

And now that they were spoken the words were not so unbelievable after all. In fact, they explained everything. The reason Julia had sung in her church choir but had never sung for us—her lack of interest in Mary Carncross's letter—the million and one little inconsistencies in personality and background that had come to light over the past months—suddenly I could understand them. It was as though the pieces of an unsolvable puzzle were coming together and suddenly, miraculously, they fit!

"But, if you're not Julia," I said softly, "then—who are you?"

"You haven't guessed that?"

"No. I can't imagine."

"My name is Sarah Blane," the girl I knew as Julia said quietly. "I worked for Ryan and Marge Grant in Pine Crest. They hired me as a cook and cleaning girl, but I realized pretty quickly that this was not the reason they wanted me to live with them. They had heard in the village that I had the gift of witchcraft handed down to me from my grandmother. They thought that if I lived with them I'd tell them things. Ryan Grant was using me to get information for his book.

"Well, that can go two ways. I used them too. While they were studying me, I studied them—the way they talked, their table manners, their outside ways. I'm smart and I can copy. By the time I'd been there a year I could do a study of Marge Grant that was so much like her that her husband himself wouldn't have known the difference in the dark. I was like the daughter of the house. I wasn't a maid, I was family."

"But Sarah Blane was killed," I said stupidly. "She was riding in the car with Aunt Marge and

Uncle Ryan when it went off the cliff. They were taking her back to the village."

"How do you know that?"

"Why, because—" Once again I paused uncertainly. "Because—"

"Because I told you so?"

"But there was a third body in the wreckage," I said. "As badly burned as they were, they were able to tell that. The third person—" And then I understood.

"It was Julia," I whispered. "The real Julia. She was the one in the car riding to the village with her parents. After the accident you took her identity. But why?"

"Me take her identity?" Sarah shook her head. "You're wrong there. Julia's the one who came back and took mine. I was the daughter in that house for a whole year, and I liked it. I wasn't about to give that place back to Julia. I wasn't going to go back to being somebody's cleaning girl, to live my whole life through in a place like Pine Crest, and marry some jakey durgen with cordwood on his breath and breed brats and slop hogs till the sky fell in. Not with a real world out there someplace waiting!"

"My aunt and uncle liked Pine Crest," I said. "They thought it was a lovely place."

"Then why did they ship their precious Julie off to Boston? They liked it, sure, for a squattin' place, for a spot for writin' a book in, but they wasn't about to stay there, you can count on that. They was goin' to leave this summer, to 'come back to civilization' as your aunt called it, and where would that of left me? Right back where I'd started, except now I knew the difference. Now I knew what it was that I was missin'."

"You didn't have to stay there," I said. "Nobody has to stay anywhere if she doesn't want to. There was nothing to stop you from taking your wages and buying a bus ticket and just—*going*."

"Just going? Where?"

"Anywhere. Any big city."

"Without schoolin'? Without trainin'? What would I do when I got there—scrub floors? What does a girl like me do, took out of school at the age of ten to help raise the little ones, whose only talent's one that nobody will pay for? Sure, I know the art of witchcraft, I learned it from my gram and her from hers, but a lot of good it would do me shut off in the hills. And in the city alone, what good there either? I'd of ended up as a waitress in some dingy little diner or being somebody's motel maid."

"Well—" I could think of no answer. There was a point to what she was saying. What could she have done? There must have been something.

"You could have gone to night school and learned a trade," I said. "Plenty of people start from nothing and make something of themselves. It takes time—"

"I got no time," Sarah said. "I spent enough time. Pine Crest was where my time went. I'm not no child no longer—"

"You're seventeen!"

"Your cousin Julie was seventeen."

"Oh!" I stared at her. "Then, you—" And another part of the puzzle fell into place. The strange, high-boned face, the womanly body, the deep knowing eyes which had seemed from the beginning so unusual for a teenage girl, were not those of a girl at all. Sarah Blane was a grown woman.

"And so," I said softly, "you decided after Julia was killed that you would take her place and come here to us. But how did you know that you could do it? What if we had known what Julia looked like, if we had guessed?"

"I was with the Grants a long time," Sarah said. "I heard a lot of things. I knew how long it was since they had seen you last and that they didn't send pictures. Like I said, I'm smart. I pick up things fast. Once I got here I learned how to act from you and your friends. It didn't take me long."

"No, it didn't," I admitted. "The clothes you wore—the dress—" I knew now where it was that I had seen the yellow dress that Sarah had worn down to dinner the first night she was with us. It was the same dress that was worn by the angel singing on the mountain top on the Grants' Christmas card. The angel had been Julia, the real Julia! No wonder the clothes had not fit correctly, had been wrong in style and color. They had been bought for an entirely different person.

"So you bought new clothes," I said, "and you got your hair cut like Carolyn's and you learned how to act like a teenager. But you must have known that you wouldn't get away with it indefinitely. When school started in the fall you would have gone in as a senior. You couldn't have done the work. There's no way you could have faked that! You'd have been found out then!"

"I am not going to be free to go to school in the fall," Sarah said calmly. "I will be needed somewhere else. There will be a home to take care of, a little boy to raise, a lonely man to be comforted.

I will have my own place then, the sort of place that should rightfully be mine. And before long the man will begin to love me and soon I will be his wife."

I stared at her in amazement.

"But I thought you were in love with Mike!"

"With Mike Gallagher?" Now it was her turn to look amazed. "You must be crazy. What would I want with a boy still wet behind the ears? Mike Gallagher—your brother Peter—I used them to learn on. The next time I make a man love me it's going to count. I will marry a man who is older and working at a good job, a man who has money and a place in the town, who can give me a nice home, my own car, clothes, all the things I need. Not a little school boy."

"And where will you find a man like that?" I asked her.

"I have found him already. This is my home," Sarah said. "I'm going to stay here."

"You mean—you can't mean—you plan to marry *Dad!*"

Of all the disclosures so far, this was the one impossible to accept. I would have laughed out loud except that there was no laughter in me.

"My father isn't available, Miss Sarah Blane! He's happily married to a woman he loves very much, and he's not going to leave her for you, no matter what charms you use on him. If there's one thing I'm sure of it's the relationship between my father and my mother. Nothing is going to break them up, absolutely nothing."

"That's probably true," Sarah said, "as long as your mother is here. But what if she isn't?"

"There's no sense to that question. She *is* here."

"This minute?"

"No, of course not. But she'll be back by noon."

"She will?"

"Certainly, she will," I said. "Why wouldn't she?"

"The Grants were coming back too. By dinner."

"The Grants—"

"There was an accident," Sarah said.

"An accident?" A chill swept over me. "You don't mean—you didn't—"

"The car swerved," Sarah said, "at a terrible place, there on a curve with a dropoff to the valley. Your uncle was a careful driver. I've wondered sometimes what he thought in that last moment when he turned the wheel and nothing happened, when the car kept on going and going and going."

"You did it?" I whispered. "You made them have that crash? But you weren't even there! You were back at the house in the hills, waiting."

"Waiting," Sarah said. "Yes, waiting."

"But that was murder!" I said incredulously.

"Was it?"

"Of course, it was. You killed three people, my aunt and uncle and cousin! That's murder if I ever heard of murder!" I was shaking with rage. "You won't get away with it either! I'll tell! I'll tell everybody!"

"Oh?" Sarah said calmly. "And who will believe you?"

"I'll start by proving that you're not Julia Grant! There are plenty of ways that that can be proved. Fingerprints, for instance, and bringing in people from the school she went to as witnesses. Mary Carncross could testify. And there are dental records. Once that is proved we're halfway toward the other. People *will* believe!"

"Do you really think I plan to let you tell them?"

"Can you stop me?"

"Of course, I can stop you. I stopped the professor, didn't I? It's a bother, I'll admit. I didn't plan to have to do it. I expected you to be in the car with your mother."

"In the car with my mother!" The full significance of the statement struck me and all the strength went out of me. My knees turned to rubber and I grabbed the edge of the shelf that held the chemical trays and leaned upon it for support. I could picture it then, the road to Santa Fe. It was filled with curves and along one side rose a bank of red clay cliffs. On the other was a sheer drop into a valley. It was the sort of road on which one drove fast if one was a good driver, a smooth, double-lane highway with one-way traffic. If a driver were confident of her car, if she did not expect it to swerve, if she was in a hurry to get home to a sick niece—

"You can't!" I breathed. "You won't! I won't let you!"

"It's a bit late for that," Sarah said. "It's already done. What do you think I was doing in my room last night with the road map? Your mother's car will leave the road at one particular spot. There is no way you can prevent it. In fact, it may already have occurred."

"It hasn't!" I cried, my voice rising to a scream. "It hasn't! It won't!" I did not stop to think what it was I was doing, I simply did it. I grabbed the tray full of stop bath in front of me and hurled the contents straight at Sarah. Her hands flew up to protect her face, and at that point I had reached the door. I plunged through it and slammed it behind me and grabbed for the padlock which Mother used when the darkroom stood vacant to keep Bobby's friends from invading the little room and using it for a clubhouse. I thrust it through the security ring and snapped it closed at exactly the instant that Sarah grabbed the door handle from the inside.

The voice that rose from the far side of the door was not the voice of a girl. I had heard that voice before on several occasions, the first of which was when it was directed at Trickle.

"You vigrous, rat-fanged varmant!" it had shrieked then. It used other words now, and they made me shudder. The person who had talked to me in the darkroom had alternated between the language of backwoods Sarah and educated Julia. Perhaps she herself had not known with certainty who she really was.

But about the cries that rose now, there could be no doubt. They came from the throat of no one but a witch.

Eighteen

Had it happened on the way up or was it to be on the return trip? This Sarah had not told me, but I could hope it was the latter for she had said, "It may already have occurred" and not "it has occurred."

I glanced at my watch. It was eleven-twenty. Mother's appointment had been at ten. There was a chance that she might still be in conference. If I could catch her before she left the magazine office I would be able to stop her.

I tore through the garage and into the kitchen, slamming the door upon the sound of the shrieking voice and pounding fists. I snatched up the receiver of the wall telephone and dialed the operator.

"*New Mexico Magazine* in Santa Fe," I told her. "I don't know the number, but it's at the Department of Development. Please hurry! It's an emergency!"

The call went through quickly. The voice that answered was young and secretarial.

"This is Rachel Bryant," I said. "My mother, Leslie Bryant, had a ten o'clock appointment with the art editor. Is she still there? It's very important that I speak with her!"

"Just a moment," the secretary said. "I'll check and see." There was a silence broken by the hum of voices rising and falling in the background. Then the secretary came back on and said, "I'm sorry. She left the office about ten minutes ago."

"Did she say where she was going?" I asked frantically. "Was she going to stop for lunch or do some shopping before she started home?"

"Let me ask," the woman said, and again there was a pause. "No," she said finally, "not that anyone here knows. She did mention that a member of the family was ill and she wanted to get back to Albuquerque as soon as possible."

"Thank you," I said and set the receiver back on the hook. What could I do now? Call Dad at work? Call Peter? Calling Dad would do no good as he had taken the bus to work so that Mother could have the car. The music store where Peter worked was halfway across town, too far for him to get home quickly even if I convinced him it was necessary.

Which left one possibility—Mike. He said he would not be working, but that did not necessarily mean that he would be home. It took me only a matter of seconds to cover the distance between our houses and press the Gallaghers' doorbell. Mike's car was in the drive, which was a good sign, for if he was out someplace he would certainly have taken the car. I pressed the bell again and began to bang on the door. What was taking him so long? Had he gone deaf?"

"Mike!" I called. "Mike!"

The door opened.

"Hey," he said, "take it easy. You don't have to knock the door down." Then he saw the expression on my face. "What's wrong?"

"I need help," I gasped.

"Something's happened at your house? Somebody's hurt?" In one long stride he was through the door and had started down the porch steps.

"No, it's out on the freeway." I clutched at his arm. "We'll need to take the car."

"Has there been an accident? Is it one of the family?"

"Come on," I begged. "There's no time for talking. You'll just have to trust me. It's terribly important. Please, Mike, believe me!"

Though, indeed, why should he? What was Mike to me at this point, or I to him?

I looked up into his face and saw bewilderment in his eyes. He would, I knew, demand an explanation. People did not go rushing off down the highway without an understanding of what was happening. He would make me stop and explain, step by step, in a logical manner. What was the problem? Who was in danger? Why did I think so? Was I some kind of nut or something?

They were the questions he might have asked, but he did not ask them. Instead he grabbed my hand and started for the car.

"Sure I believe you," he said. "Where do we go?"

"Onto the freeway," I told him, "and north toward Santa Fe."

"Right." He threw open the car door, shoved me in and slid in behind me. Thrusting the key into the ignition, he started the car and backed out of the driveway. I glanced back at the house and saw Mrs. Gallagher standing in the doorway, a look of surprise on her round, motherly face. She took a step forward as Mike slammed the car into first and brought his foot down upon the accelerator. Her mouth opened, and although I could not hear her I could read the words: "Where are you two going?"

The car leapt forward. Mike took the corner at the end of the street and put us onto Louisiana Avenue. The light in front of us was red. We went straight through it. Several cars blew their horns at us as we shot past them. A ramp lay to the right, and we sped onto it and around the sloping curve that brought us onto the freeway. The road led west and then it curved once more and at last we were headed north with the highway straight and smooth before us and the land stretched flat to the mountains on either side.

"Now," Mike said. "Can you tell me where we're going and why?"

"It's Mother," I said, wondering how much he would be able to accept. "We've got to intercept her. She's going to have an accident."

"You mean there's something wrong with her car?"

"Well—yes."

"What sort of thing?"

"It's the steering," I said. "The car is going to swerve."

"How do you know?"

"I just—do."

"How?" He glanced over at me. "You've got to be basing this on something. What makes you think the steering's going to blow?"

I drew a deep breath. "Julia told me."

"Julia? How does she know? Julia doesn't know anything about cars."

"Mike," I said, "you told me you believed me. Please trust me and I promise I'll explain it all later. I can't even think right now about anything except Mother. If we're late—if we don't reach her in time—" I let the sentence fade off, unable to complete it.

"Do you know she's left Santa Fe already?"

"I checked right before coming over to your house. She had finished her business conference ten minutes before. That means she could be a third of the way home by now." I forced myself to say the words. I did not want to face them. A third of the way home would mean that she was already driving in the area of the cliffs.

"Not necessarily," Mike said. "You know what the parking is like around the plaza in the summertime. She might have had to put her car in a lot. That would mean it could take twenty minutes or so for her to walk back to it and get paid up and out on the road."

"Can we go faster?" I begged.

"We're at the top of the speed limit now."

"Please, Mike, go faster!"

Mike, who had never broken a law in his life, glanced in the rearview mirror and bore down on the gas pedal. We passed the turnoff to the Indian pueblo so quickly that I never saw it flash by. I closed my eyes and tried to send my mind flying ahead of the car. Mother, I screamed silently, pull

off the road and stop! Wait for us—wait for us! I
knew she would not hear me. It was Julia, not I,
who could do things with her mind.

No, not Julia, but *Sarah*. I had never known
Julia, the laughing, joking, singing Julie who had
been my cousin. That Julie had gone to church
and worn yellow dresses and played the guitar. She
had been seventeen with her life still in front of
her. There was a boy named Dick Carncross who
was eager to meet her; he liked her picture. Perhaps she would have liked him also if she had met
him. Perhaps they would even have fallen in love.
Seventeen years old with never a chance to be
eighteen! Oh, Julie, I thought, you were cheated!
You never had a chance for anything! And I
wanted to cry for the girl I had not known and
now would never ever know.

I opened my eyes and found we had left the flat
land behind us. The road was steadily rising and
the terrain was changing. We were into the hills
and the curves and dips, and the earth had lost its
dust color and was growing red with clay content.
The sky seemed bluer and the air clearer.

"How much further?" I asked.

"To the heart of Santa Fe?"

"To the cliffs. How far to the cliffs?"

"We're almost into them," Mike said. "You can
see how the land's getting craggy. You still won't
tell me?"

"I can't until we find her!" The road was no
longer straight, it was winding and the hills on the
sides were growing higher. "There's a place," I
said, "where the bank drops off. It's a sort of canyon. Not really deep but—deep enough."

"Is that where we're headed?"

"Yes." My hands were clenched in my lap. "How much further is it?"

"Not far at all. We're almost to it."

"That's where—" I broke off as the car began to jerk. "What is it? What's happening? You're slowing down!"

"It's the gas," Mike said. "It's acting like it's out of gas. I don't understand it. I filled the tank yesterday. There must be a leak in the tank or—"

"We can't stop now!"

"I'm sorry," Mike said. "There's nothing I can do about it." He twisted the wheel to the right and guided us onto the shoulder. The car lurched and coughed and sputtered and the engine went silent. We rolled a few yards and came to a stop.

I threw open the door and jumped out.

"Hey, come back here!" Mike shouted.

I did not answer. My eyes were focussed on the curve up ahead. "We're almost to it," Mike had told me. Beyond that curve was the place that I was headed. You've done your job, Sarah, I thought wretchedly. You've really done it! A leak in the gas tank!

I began to run and after a moment I realized that Mike was running beside me. How long we ran I do not know for after a while we reached a point where there was no such thing as time. There was only my pounding heart and the blazing heat of the sun on my head and the thud of my feet as they struck the road. I could not seem to get enough air into my lungs. The heat shimmered on the road like rippling pools of black water moving always a little ahead of us, and I knew we would never get there until it was done.

It was late, too late. As I rounded the curve I knew what I would see. Swerve marks on the road. A gaping hole in the guardrail. A blazing car in the ravine. How could I have thought to defeat it? It would have to be. Sarah had planned it and Sarah did not make mistakes.

But I was wrong, for that was not the scene that greeted me. The rail was intact and there was no sign of an accident. There was only a stretch of road that I knew well, so well, and as I recognized it I knew, too, what was to happen in the next few minutes.

There had been a dream in which I was running along a winding road. There were stark, red cliffs on one side of me and on the other there was a dropoff. My legs ached and my breath was coming in gasps, and I cried to Mike who was running beside me, "Will we get there in time? Can we get there before it happens?"

He said, "Are you crazy, Rae? If you'd only explain—"

"I can't!" I cried. "There's no time!"

Up ahead, far, far ahead, a tiny reflection of the noonday sunlight signalled the approach of a car coming toward us down the road.

"Stop!" I screamed. "Stop!" And as in the dream, I ran straight into the middle of the road with my arms outspread. The car came roaring toward me, and I was able to look directly into the eyes of the driver, wide, familiar eyes that recognized me as I did them. I could see Mother's face as she hit the brake, a white face blank with amazement. The car went past me and then it began to swerve. Like a child's windup toy with faulty steering it moved in a steady line toward the dropoff and came to a stop a matter of inches from the edge.

There was a moment of dead silence. Then, as from far away, there came into my head the sound of singing, high and joyful and sweet. Faint and far, a ringing in my ears, part of the dizziness of relief, or something else? Angel Julie singing?

I didn't know. It didn't matter. What did matter was that we had, after all, made it in time. Mike's arm was around my shoulders and Mother was opening the car door and getting out.

"My Lord," she said shakily. "The steering cable must have snapped. If I hadn't seen you and started to slow down before it happened—" She glanced at the dropoff and shuddered. "What in the world are you two doing here? When I saw Rae running up the highway I couldn't believe my eyes!"

"I don't know," Mike said. "Rae knew, somehow, about the car."

"It's been so long," I said. "I called the magazine office. They said you left there a little after eleven. It's almost twelve-thirty now. You should have reached this spot a long time ago." Something had delayed her. That was obvious. Something had been working for us, something that Sarah, with all her powers, could not defeat or control.

"What was it?" I asked. "Why did you take so long?"

"I stopped," Mother said, "to get you a present. I told you there was something I was planning to get you."

She gestured toward the car window and I looked in and saw it, there in the back seat—the clownish white face, the cocked ears, the friendly, inquisitive brown eyes. It was a miniature of Trickle.

"This has been such a difficult summer for you, honey," Mother said, "I thought it might help to have your own dog again. Not that he will ever replace Trickle—you don't replace a person—but he can make his own place in your life. All of us in the family have been so worried about you. We hate to see you so unhappy."

And there in her eyes was the answer, the thing Sarah had not reckoned on, had not been prepared to handle, had not known how to combat.

It was love.

Once more it is summer. Golden summer.

I stand on the front lawn with the morning paper. The dog, Lucky—(at four years old he can hardly be termed a "puppy")—rolls around in the grass at my feet, begging to be played with. The sun is warm on my hair and on the back of my neck as I stand reading the article in section C. There are often such articles. There was a time when I skipped over them, hardly noticing they were there. But for the last four years I have read them carefully, paying attention to every detail.

A family lost in the mountains. An unidentified "girl friend" of the daughter's, lost with them. Their camper truck and belongings missing. Who, I wonder, is the girl friend? Is she involved in the tragedy—or might she have created it? There is a photograph of the family but this girl is not in it. Was she the one who held the camera? Or did someone else take the picture, and was this girl one of the group who was photographed, and did the image somehow not emerge when the negative was developed?

"That part I cannot accept," the professor told me. "It's pure superstition."

"But I found her destroying the film before it could be developed!"

"That proves nothing except that Sarah herself believed her image would not be there. She was taking no chances. If the film had been processed I would guess she would have been on it. Still, who knows?"

There are so many things we cannot know. Was Sarah a real witch or did she just believe she was?

My father thinks the latter.

"There are reasonable explanations for everything," he says. "The steering failure in two cars could have been a strange coincidence. Hives can be caused by nerves. A dog can be poisoned. Teenage boys are often infatuated by girls who are different from those they are used to knowing; such romances seldom last but can be very intense. Gas tanks can leak. An elderly man can have a stroke and partial recovery."

"But the recovery began so immediately upon Sarah's leaving!"

"It could have been psychological. Just knowing she was gone could have given him the will to get better."

She was gone when we got back to the house. It was Bobby who had released her from the darkroom.

"She kept yelling for me to help her," he said. "How could I know I shouldn't unlock the door? She said Rae was playing a joke and had shut her in there. When she came out she went to her room and got her things and left. She didn't say where she was going."

So we cannot know. We can only assume that she is somewhere, entwining herself in the lives of those she meets, using them as she can to gain the things she wants.

Sarah!

Julia!

And so I stand now on the front lawn, reading, and behind me the door of the house opens. It is a duplex, part of the student housing at the edge of the university campus, much smaller than the house in which I used to live with my parents and brothers. I turn and lower the paper and smile at the blue-eyed man who stands in the doorway.

"Hey, Red," he calls. "How about fixing breakfast? Have you forgotten that summer classes start early?"

"No, Mike, I haven't forgotten," I say laughing. "Isn't it about time though that you learned how to fry an egg?"

I stick the paper under my arm and whistle for Lucky, and we head for the house. For too long now I've dwelt upon the past. One cannot live indefinitely with shadows. The summer of fear lies well behind us. It is a time now of new beginnings.